782.1402 M491A 2009
Peter Rodgers Melnick
Adrift in Macao

# Adrift In Macao

## Book & Lyrics by
## Christopher Durang

## Music by
## Peter Melnick

D0707277

A SAMUEL FRENCH ACTING EDITION

# SAMUEL FRENCH

FOUNDED 1830

NEW YORK HOLLYWOOD LONDON TORONTO

SAMUELFRENCH.COM

Copyright © 2009 by Christopher Durang & Peter Melnick

ALL RIGHTS RESERVED

Cover image Copyright © 2009 by Primary Stages

CAUTION: Professionals and amateurs are hereby warned that *ADRIFT IN MACAO* is subject to a Licensing Fee. It is fully protected under the copyright laws of the United States of America, the British Commonwealth, including Canada, and all other countries of the Copyright Union. All rights, including professional, amateur, motion picture, recitation, lecturing, public reading, radio broadcasting, television and the rights of translation into foreign languages are strictly reserved. In its present form the play is dedicated to the reading public only.

The amateur live stage performance rights to *ADRIFT IN MACAO* are controlled exclusively by Samuel French, Inc., and licensing arrangements and performance licenses must be secured well in advance of presentation. PLEASE NOTE that amateur Licensing Fees are set upon application in accordance with your producing circumstances. When applying for a licensing quotation and a performance license please give us the number of performances intended, dates of production, your seating capacity and admission fee. Licensing Fees are payable one week before the opening performance of the play to Samuel French, Inc., at 45 W. 25th Street, New York, NY 10010.

Licensing Fee of the required amount must be paid whether the play is presented for charity or gain and whether or not admission is charged.

Stock licensing fees quoted upon application to Samuel French, Inc.

For all other rights than those stipulated above, apply to: Patrick Herold c/o Helen Merrill, LLC, 295 Lafayette Street, Suite 915, New York, NY 10012.

Particular emphasis is laid on the question of amateur or professional readings, permission and terms for which must be secured in writing from Samuel French, Inc.

Copying from this book in whole or in part is strictly forbidden by law, and the right of performance is not transferable.

Whenever the play is produced the following notice must appear on all programs, printing and advertising for the play: "Produced by special arrangement with Samuel French, Inc."

Due authorship credit must be given on all programs, printing and advertising for the play.

ISBN 978-0-573-66309-3          Printed in U.S.A.          #3829

No one shall commit or authorize any act or omission by which the copyright of, or the right to copyright, this play may be impaired.

No one shall make any changes in this play for the purpose of production.

Publication of this play does not imply availability for performance. Both amateurs and professionals considering a production are strongly advised in their own interests to apply to Samuel French, Inc., for written permission before starting rehearsals, advertising, or booking a theatre.

No part of this book may be reproduced, stored in a retrieval system, or transmitted in any form, by any means, now known or yet to be invented, including mechanical, electronic, photocopying, recording, videotaping, or otherwise, without the prior written permission of the publisher.

## IMPORTANT BILLING AND CREDIT REQUIREMENTS

All producers of *ADRIFT IN MACAO* *must* give credit to the Author of the Play in all programs distributed in connection with performances of the Play, and in all instances in which the title of the Play appears for the purposes of advertising, publicizing or otherwise exploiting the Play and/or a production. The name of the Author *must* appear on a separate line on which no other name appears, immediately following the title and *must* appear in size of type not less than fifty percent of the size of the title type.

"ADRIFT IN MACAO"
Book and Lyrics by Christopher Durang
Music by Peter Melnick
The following credits shall appear on the presentation page in the acting edition of the Work and shall be required to be given by licensees on a separate line, in a size of at least 15% of the size of the title, on the main credit page of all programs for stage productions of the Work in the United States and Canada:
The New York Premiere of "Adrift in Macao" was
Produced by Primary Stages in New York City, January 2007
(Casey Childs founder and Executive Producer, Andrew Leynett, Artistic Director, Elliot Fox, Managing Director)

Originally presented by New York Stage and Film Company
And the Powerhouse Theater at Vassar on July 10, 2002

Licensees shall be required to give the following credit (in size and prominence of type no less than that used for the designers' credit) on the main credit page of all theatre programs when Michael Starobin's orchestrations are utilized:

Orchestrations
By
Michael Starobin

*ADRIFT IN MACAO* was given its premiere New York City production January 23, 2007 at Primary Stages (Casey Childs, Founder and Executive Producer; Andrew Leynse, Artistic Director; Elliot Fox, Managing Director) in association with Ina Meibach, Susan Dietz, Jennifer Manocherian, Barbara Manocherian. The Associate Producer was Jamie deRoy and the Associate Artistic Director was Michelle Bossy.

The production was directed by Sheryl Kaller with musical direction by Fred Lassen, choreography by Christopher Gatelli, sets by Thomas Lynch, costumes by Willa Kim, lighting by Jeff Croiter, orchestrations by Michael Starobin, and sound by Peter Fitzgerald. Casting was by Mark Simon. Production Supervision was provided by PRF Productions. The music coordinator was Howard Joines, the music copyist was Anne Kaye and Kaye-Houston Music. Props were provided by R. Jay Duckworth. Charlie Corcoran was the associate set designer. Tara Wilkinson was the assistant choreographer, and Andy Sandberg was the assistant to the director. Leanne Mahoney was the assistant costume designer, Grant Yaeger was the assistant lighting designer, Megan Hanniger was the associate sound designer. Wigs were provided by Tom Watson. The Press Representative was O & M. The production stage manager was Emily Wells, with Robyn Henry as the Assistant Stage Manager. The cast was as follows:

LUREENA . . . . . . . . . . . . . . . . . . . . . . . . . . . . . . . . . . . . . Rachel de Benedet
MITCH. . . . . . . . . . . . . . . . . . . . . . . . . . . . . . . . . . . . . . . . . Alan Campbell
TEMPURA . . . . . . . . . . . . . . . . . . . . . . . . . . . . . . . . . . . . .Orville Mendoza
CORINNA . . . . . . . . . . . . . . . . . . . . . . . . . . . . . . . . . . . . . Michelle Ragusa
RICK . . . . . . . . . . . . . . . . . . . . . . . . . . . . . . . . . . . . . . . . . . . .Will Swenson
TRENCHCOAT CHORUS . . . . . . . . . . .Jonathan Rayson, Elisa Van Duyne
JOE THE BARTENDER . . . . . . . . . . . . . . . . . . . . . . . . . . . .Jonathan Rayson
DAISY THE CIGARETTE GIRL . . . . . . . . . . . . . . . . . . . . . Elisa Van Duyne

Prior to the Primary Stages production, the first reading of the musical was done in the York Theatre Developmental Series in New York City. Its first production was by the New York Stage And Film Company and the Powerhouse Theatre at Vassar on July 10, 2002. Its second production was at the Philadelphia Theatre Company on October 19, 2005, where it received several Barrymore Award nominations, winning three for Ms. de Benedet, Ms. Ragusa, and Mr. Mendoza for their performances.

# CAST

**LUREENA**
**MITCH**
**CORINNA**
**TEMPURA**
**RICK**
**TRENCHCOAT CHORUS** (1 male, 1 female)

**NOTE:** The Trenchcoat Chorus is a chorus of two, a young man and young woman, who show up from time to time to perform in some of the musical numbers. The young man also plays Joe the bartender, and the young woman plays Daisy, the cigarette girl.

In the prologue they play multiple parts. The man plays the Chinese person in coolie hat. The two of them play the three couples who embark from the ship in quick succession (and with quick, playful costume changes). And finally the man plays The Man Expecting to Meet Someone, and the woman plays the Worldly Woman.

## TIME

1952

## PLACE

Macao, China

The musical is presented without an intermission.

## MUSICAL NUMBERS

Prologue . . . . . . . . . . . . . . . . . . . . . . . . . . . . . . . . . . . . . . . . . . The Company

In a Foreign City . . . . . . . . . . . . . . . . . . . . . . . . . . . . . . . . . . . . . . Lureena

Reprise: In a Foreign City (In a Grumpy Mood . . . . . . . . . . . . . . . . Mitch

Tempura's Song . . . . . . . . . . . . . . . . . . . . . . . . . . . . . . . . . . . . . . . Tempura

Mister McGuffin . . . . . . . . . . . . . . . . . . . . . . . . . . . . . . . Corinna, Tempura,

Trenchcoat Chorus

Pretty Moon Over Macao . . . . . . . . . . . . . . . . . . . . . . . . . . . . . . Lureena

Mambo Malaysian . . . . . . . . . . . . . . . . . . . . . . . . . . . . . . . . . . . . . Corinna

Pretty Moon/Mambo Malaysian . . . . . . . . . . . . . . . . . . . Lureena, Corinna

Sparks . . . . . . . . . . . . . . . . . . . . . . . . . . . . . . . . . . . . . . . . Lureena, Mitch

Adrift in Macao . . . . . . . . . . . . . . . . . Mitch, Lureena, Corinna, Tempura

So Long . . . . . . . . . . . . . . . . . . . . . . . . . . . . . . . . . . . . . . . . . . . . Lureena

Rick's Song . . . . . . . . . . . . . . . . . . . . . . . . . . . . . . . . . . . . . . . . . . . . . Rick

(**NOTE:** This song is not normally listed in the program
because it's meant to surprise the audience)

The Chase . . . . . . . . . . . . . . . . . . . . . . . . . . . . . . . Mitch and the Company

Revelation . . . . . . . . . . . . . . . . . . . . . . . . . . . . . . . . . . . . . . . . . . . Tempura

Ticky, Ticky, Tock . . . . . . . . . . . . Lureena, Corinna, Trenchcoat Chorus;

Tempura (later)

# SYNOPSIS OF SCENES

# PROLOGUE

*In the dark, the orchestra plays an opening "fanfare" which sounds like the MGM or 20th Century Fox musical introductions to their movies (though performed live). At the end of the fanfare, the fanfare is musically punctuated by a gong. The gong is struck by* **TEMPURA**, *lit by spotlight. He is dressed in Asian garb and is often exaggeratedly subservient, but also full of many other emotional colors. But that's for later. Right now, he is just hitting a gong. And then he scurries off.*

*Lights up on stage. We are at the docks of Macao, China, at the wharf. The Macao of this musical is the Macao (and China) of Hollywood movies, so don't worry about authenticity. It's an imagined Macao, dark and dangerous, and glamorous too.*

*There are docks upstage, and a gang plank leading down from them. Perhaps the sounds of gulls in the distance; definitely a ship's whistle.*

**A MAN IN A WHITE SUIT** *and hat stands with his back to us.*

*The man turns around. It is* **RICK.** *He looks off-stage and signals to someone.*

**TEMPURA** *comes in, bowed and deferential to* **RICK.** *He has a pitter-patter kind of walk.*

**RICK** *takes the object part-way out of the bag to show* **TEMPURA** *– it is a Maltese Falcon.* **TEMPURA** *nods.*

**RICK** *puts the Falcon back into the bag, and hands it to* **TEMPURA.**

**TEMPURA** *scurries off-stage.*

**RICK** *looks around, he checks his watch, he has another appointment still. He exits with purpose.*

*A woman comes on, walking with exaggerated secrecy, as if she thinks if she walks slowly and creeps no one will see her. This is* **CORINNA**. *She is wearing a raincoat (or something that covers her core costume).*

*She gets to right of center, and looks around, worried. She's to meet someone.*

**A CHINESE PERSON** *with a coolie hat half-walks, half-runs in and over to* **CORINNA**. *He hands her a small packet of something, she hands him some money. He looks at the money quickly, it's ok, and he scurries off.*

*The transaction finished,* **CORINNA** *stands up straight and now walks off-stage with a normal gait, as if she's just walking home from the supermarket (or something very respectable and average). She exits.*

*(Note: a man and a woman play the* **TRENCHCOAT CHORUS** *in the musical, and they play the extra roles in the Prologue. Thus* **TRENCHCOAT MAN** *is dressed as the* **CHINESE PERSON** *with a coolie hat.)*

*The distinct sound of a boat whistle.*

*The music becomes less mysterious here — more "oh something interesting is happening."*

*We hear a* **VOICE** *over the sound system:*

**VOICE.** *(In Chinese:)* Gai sia juan dad au sia juan.

*(Pronounced: "guy see-oh twon duh doe see-ah twon)*

*(The above is a phonetic breakdown Chinese for "All ashore who's going ashore".)*

**VOICE.** *(cont.) (Then in English, with Chinese accent:)* All ashore who's going ashore.

*The music shifts to something jaunty, and passengers start to enter upstage onto the dock, and then walk down the gang plank.*

*Most of the passengers are played by the* **TRENCHCOAT MAN** *and* **TRENCHCOAT WOMAN**, *who keep changing costumes with dizzying quickness off-stage. The changes in the costume can be silly and slapdash if you want, as long as we know they're different people.*

*First we see a* **HAPPY COUPLE**, *both carrying suitcases. She wears a distinctive hat, and he wears a fedora. They walk down the gang plank, excited and happy to be there. They exit downstage left.*

*Next we see* **MITCH BOONTON**. *He carries a beat-up suitcase. He is masculine and rugged; he is also existentially tired. He is running from something. Or to something. In any case, he's a bit brooding. He stands on the dock, looks around a second to get his bearings.*

*While* **MITCH** *stands there, a* **SECOND COUPLE** − *once again played by our* **TRENCHCOAT CHORUS** *duo − enters on to the upstage platform and heads down the gang plank.* **MITCH** *has to get out of their way.*

*We should let it be a joke that we just saw this couple a second ago − and the costume differences should be noticeable but also minor. The* **WOMAN** *wears a different hat. The* **MAN** *is maybe bareheaded. Their luggage is different. If in their previous entrance, she was on his left, we now reverse that, and she's on his right. They also have a different attitude. Maybe they're sour that they're there. Maybe they're tired. Maybe the man is dominating, and the woman is carrying the bags. Or maybe they're just wondering and gaga at being abroad. You decide.*

*They walk down the gang plank, and exit off-stage.*

**MITCH** *is now alone on the dock. The music changes for him, a bit moody. He walks down the gang plank. If this were a movie, he'd get a close-up. In any case, he should stop and look out front for a moment, lost in thought and bit gloomy. He thinks. Then he goes off stage right.*

*The jaunty/happy music starts again, and now there is a* **THIRD COUPLE** − *our duo again, and with more tiny costume changes. I'm not sure what their new attitude might be. They could have a guide book, and be checking it? Maybe they could both be limping? Or they're taking pictures of one another? Up for discussion. They go down the gang plank and exit.*

*Now* **LUREENA** *enters onto the dock.*

*The music "features" her, she is our leading lady.*

*She's in a glamorous evening gown. Very unsuitable for travel. And she has no luggage. She is very attractive. And also a bit jaded. She's been disappointed a lot, especially in love.*

*She stands at the top of the gang plank, looking around her, getting her bearings. She looks out, wondering what Macao has in store for her. As with* **MITCH***'s moment a little bit ago, this is her "close up."*

*Our* **TRENCHCOAT MAN** *now enters from the same place the* **COUPLES** *have. But he is by himself. He's wearing a raincoat, a different fedora. He maybe has no luggage. He is* **THE MAN EXPECTING TO MEET SOMEONE** *at the dock. He stands at the top of the gang plank. He looks around.* **LUREENA** *watches him.*

*From off-stage, a* **WORLDLY WOMAN** *enters. Played by our* **TRENCHCOAT WOMAN***, she is dressed like Barbara Stanwyck in her recognizable look from the film noir classic "Double Indemnity" – she has a platinum wig on, a beige or white raincoat, sunglasses, and a blank expression. She sort of stops in place, and stares out. The music turns noir-ish here, with a vague sense of danger.*

*The* **MAN** *on the dock sees her, waves, and runs down the gang plank to her. They embrace and kiss.*

**LUREENA** *watches them, thinking how lucky to be in love. They finish their kiss, and exit.*

**LUREENA** *refocuses on her own life, and now starts to walk down the gang plank.*

*She stops mid-plank when the music turns suddenly darker, more threatening. She looks off-stage and sees something that makes her back up quickly on the gang plank.*

*The* **MAN** *comes running back on-stage from downstage left. The* **WORLDLY WOMAN** *follows, not running, but with focus. She is holding a gun; she extends her arm and shoots the* **MAN** *repeatedly.*

*He seems stunned, and then – as if on a delay – he reacts to the bullets, which make his body "jerk" off-stage right. (Thus he dies off-stage.)*

*The noir music has been building, and it climaxes at the gunshot.*

**LUREENA** *is shocked to have witnessed a murder.*

*The* **WORLDLY WOMAN** *walks off-stage in a calm manner, and is gone.*

*We look back at* **LUREENA**. *Her face registers a bit of shock and "Lord, where have I just come to?" She frowns and makes a "goodness!" sort of face. Then she decides it's not really her business, she has her own problems. She sort of shakes off what she just saw, and now walks down the gang plank.*

**LUREENA** *looks glamorous indeed as she walks down the gang plank. She walks to the edge of the stage.*

**MITCH** *now comes back on, still with his suitcase. Maybe he went in the wrong direction, and has retraced his steps. He is upstage of* **LUREENA**, *and as he crosses the stage, though he can't quite see her face, he finds himself stopping to look at her.*

*She senses him and looks toward him too. But then looks away. They manage never to look at each other at the same time.* **MITCH** *looks back again, thinks for a moment, but has a "better not, I get in trouble with women" look on his face, and he continues crossing off-stage.*

**LUREENA** *senses he's gone, but "what does it matter." She has to start surviving here in Macao. She looks forward to where the street is, and holds up her hand.*

**LUREENA.** Rickshaw! Rickshaw!

(*None of the rickshaws stop for her.*)

**LUREENA.** Rickshaw!

(**RICK,** *who we saw before with the Maltese Falcon, approaches her.*)

**RICK.** Hello, I'm Rick Shaw.

**LUREENA.** No, no, I mean rickshaw boys. Chinese taxis.

**RICK.** Oh, sorry.

**LUREENA.** I just witnessed a murder.

**RICK.** Yes, well the docks at Macao can be dangerous. See you around, I hope.

**LUREENA.** Well, it's a small cast.

(**RICK** *exits. A spotlight hits* **LUREENA.** *She sings.*)

**LUREENA.**

IN A FOREIGN CITY
IN A SLINKY DRESS,
THE WEATHER'S LOOKIN' STORMY,
AND MY HAIR IS QUITE A MESS,
I LOST MY LOVER BILLY
UNLUCKY ME, I GUESS,
NOW I'M IN A FOREIGN CITY
IN A SLINKY DRESS

MY OTHER CLOTHES ARE GONE NOW
THE HOTEL KEPT THEM ALL,
CAUSE BILLY TOOK OUR MONEY,
I GUESS I TOOK A FALL,
WHEN BILLY SAID TO KISS HIM,
OH WHY DID I SAY YES?
NOW I'M IN A FOREIGN CITY
IN A SLINKY DRESS.

GOT BAD TASTE
CHOOSING A LOVER
I SURE CAN PICK 'EM
IT'S SIMPLY INSANE

WHEN IT'S TIME
TO RUN FOR COVER
I'M LIKE A FOOL WHO THINKS IT'S SUNNY
WHEN IT'S POURING RAIN

*(Thunder, lightning.* **RICK** *comes back and holds a small umbrella above her head.)*

**LUREENA.** Thank you.

*(sings)*

I'M IN A FOREIGN CITY
IN A SLINKY DRESS,
THE RICKSHAW BOYS IGNORE ME,
SO WHAT, I COULD CARE LESS,
I NEED A JOB TOMORROW,
I'M SCARED I MUST CONFESS,
SCARED TO BE...
IN A FOREIGN CITY
IN A SLINKY DRESS
A SLINKY DRESS....SLINKY DRESS.

*(A clap of lightning maybe coincides with the last chord. The rain stops, it becomes brighter.)*

**LUREENA.** Oh, the sun's come out. How convenient. And I thought it was night.

**RICK.** It is night. That's just the moon. Welcome to Macao.

**LUREENA.** Thank you.

**RICK.** I heard you sing that you needed a job.

**LUREENA.** You were listening to my singing?

**RICK.** Well, I was standing next to you.

**LUREENA.** Some things are private. But maybe it's just as well. I'm a nightclub singer, do you know where I could get a job?

**RICK.** You mean as a prostitute?

**LUREENA.** No, as a singer.

**RICK.** As it happens, I have a nightclub/gambling casino; and I could use a nightclub singer.

**LUREENA.** Every country I go to I manage to get a job as a nightclub singer. I don't know how I do it.

RICK. You're beautiful.

LUREENA. Now, let's get one thing clear. I may be beautiful and even oversexed, but business is business, and never the twain shall meet.

RICK. Which twain?

LUREENA. The gwavy twain.

RICK. What?

LUREENA. I don't know what I said. Forget it. Why are you here at this time of night? You said the docks are dangerous.

RICK. I'm not afraid of danger. I like it. Plus I had to meet a…business acquaintance.

LUREENA. You make it sound shady.

RICK. Bright sunlight is not good for some business. Shade is better.

LUREENA. Uh huh.

RICK. Plus I was supposed to have a second appointment… with a Mr. McGuffin.

LUREENA. Oh, how odd.

RICK. Why, do you know him?

LUREENA. No. But did you know Alfred Hitchcock says that the plots of his films are just excuses for suspense, and he calls these plots "the McGuffin"?

RICK. Uh….No, I didn't know that.

LUREENA. Well, he does. I dated a French film critic in Marseille for awhile, and they love American B movies there, and they call them "film noir" which is French for…"black and white movie set at night, with danger and guns and glamorous women in evening gowns."

RICK. You're full of information.

LUREENA. I get around. Now what about this job you're offering me? Are you on the level?

RICK. Not entirely. But I am offering you a job. Come on. Let me take you to my casino, the Macao Surf and Turf Nightclub Gambling Casino.

LUREENA. That's a pretty long name.

**RICK.** And it's a long walk. We better take a rickshaw. Oh, rickshaw, rickshaw!

**LUREENA.** This is where I came in, isn't it?

*(They go off. Tech note: The gang plank may be taken off, and the lighting implies a different location, though probably nearby.)*

*(**MITCH** comes back in. He 38-45, very masculine, sure of himself, a little bored with life. He's carrying only one small bag. Maybe thunder again. He sings.)*

**MITCH.**

> IN A FOREIGN CITY
> IN A GRUMPY MOOD,
> I'VE JUST ARRIVED FROM SOMEWHERE
> NEED A PLACE AND NEED SOME FOOD,
> DON'T CARRY TOO MUCH WITH ME
> IT'S OKAY SLEEPIN' NUDE,
> BUT THAT'S TOO MUCH INFORMATION
> FOR A GRUMPY MOOD
>
> CAN'T GO HOME
> SO I MUST WANDER,
> AS TO THE REASON
> I DON'T WANT TO SAY
>
> TRAVELIN' THROUGH
> HERE, THERE AND YONDER
> TRAVELIN' IS FINE BUT GEE I'M MISSIN'
> THE GOOD OL' U.S.A.
>
> IN A FOREIGN CITY
> IN A GRUMPY MOOD,
> I NEED SOME RELAXATION
> NEED TO STARE A BIT AND BROOD,
> IT'S RAINING, I'VE A HEADACHE
> AND I'VE GOT AN ATTITUDE
> CAUSE I'M IN A FOREIGN CITY
> IN A SLINKY DRESS,
> I MEAN, A GRUMPY MOOD
> A GRUMPY, GROUCHY MOO-OOD....

*(Lights shift on the stage.)*

## Scene 2
*(but the action is continuous)*

*(A small area lights up, and* **TEMPURA**, *the Asian character we've seen earlier, is revealed sitting. He holds a dangling small ball in front of himself, and stares at it, seemingly about to hypnotize himself.)*

*(***MITCH*** crosses over to* **TEMPURA**.*)*

**MITCH.** Excuse me. I'm Mitch Boonton. I'm an expatriate American, 38 to 45, very masculine, sure of myself and a little bored with life. Tell me – is this Rick Shaw's Macao Surf and Turf Nightclub Gambling Casino?

**TEMPURA.** Wait a minute.

*(continues to twirl the ball in front of himself)*

You are getting sleepy, you are getting very sleepy. At the count of 2, you are in a deep sleep. One, two…

*(He falls asleep.)*

**MITCH.** Hey, I asked you a question. You there? Hey, Asian person.

**TEMPURA.** *(wakes up)* What is, what is? Can you not see I was sleeping?

**MITCH.** What are you, trying to reinforce the stereotype of the inscrutable Asian?

**TEMPURA.** I am not inscrutable. I am very scrutable. Look at how scrutable I am. Now I'm happy. *(big smile)* Now I'm sad. *(looks sad)*. Now I'm scared. *(looks scared)* That was not inscrutable, was it? You were able to scrute me.

**MITCH.** Yeah, I guess so. I'm looking for Mr. Rick Shaw. Do you know where he is?

**TEMPURA.** Hmmmm…maybe yes, maybe no.

**MITCH.** Sounds pretty inscrutable to me.

**TEMPURA.** *(angry)* A-koo, a-koo! Sha-pie-a koo-puttibuh.

**MITCH.** How'd you like a knuckle sandwich?

**TEMPURA.** *(sings)*

> GOODNESS! GRACIOUS!
> WHY YOU WANT TO TALK TO ME SO ROUGH AND
> TOUGH?
>
> KNUCKLE SANDWICH!??
> WHO WANT SANDWICH MADE OF FIST?
> YANKEE, NEED TO COOL DOWN

**MITCH.** Look, I'm sorry.

**TEMPURA.** Shut up! I see pattern.

> *(continues singing)*
>
> INSIST YOU GET YOUR OWN WAY
> JUST BECAUSE AMERICAN,
> YOU THINK YOU CHIEF
> IS IT THEIR DIET?
> PORK AND VEAL AND BEEF

**MITCH.** What?

**TEMPURA.** *(sings)*

> AMERICANS ARE VIOLENT
> AMERICANS ARE ROWDY,
> ALWAYS KNOCKING DOORS DOWN
> ALWAYS CRACKING HEADS,
> WHY CAN'T YOU BE PEACEFUL
> LIKE LOVELY LOTUS LEAF,
> AMERICANS ARE NASTY
> THEY EAT A LOT OF BEEF
>
> HAMBURGER, HAMBURGER
> FRIES AND SLAW,
> BLOODY OLD ROAST BEEF,
> THEY NIBBLE ON AND GNAW
> DISGUSTING, DISGUSTING,
> THEY NEED TO EAT FISH RAW
>
> AMERICANS ARE FILTHY,
> NASTY, VILE AND VICIOUS,
> FEET AS BIG AS MOUNTAIN,
> BRAIN AS SMALL AS PEA,
> WHY CAN'T YOU BE GRACIOUS

LIKE TEA OF AUGUST MOON,
I WISH YOU'D LEARN SOME MANNERS
OR HOPE YOU DIE REAL SOON

AM I ANTI-AMERICAN?
NO, NO, WELL, A LITTLE

BUT YOU ALL ARE SUCH PIGS,
AND YOU EAT PIG
YUCK, BLEGGGGHHH, VOMIT!
COCA COLA, POTATO CHIP,
BAD FOOD, MAKES ME...
YUCK, BLEGGGGHHH, VOMIT!

STILL I BEND LIKE THE REED,
LET US PRETEND TO BE FRIENDS,

HAVE YOU GOT A CHOCOLATE BAR FOR TEMPURA?
    WOULD YOU LIKE TO BUY A PROSTITUTE?
HAVE YOU GOT A CIGARETTE FOR TEMPURA?
    WOULD YOU LIKE TO BUY A PROSTITUTE?

**MITCH.** Is that the end of your song? I found it rambling, offensive and, yes, inscrutable.

**TEMPURA.** Okay, boss.

**MITCH.** Boss?

**TEMPURA.** Every American in Macao is my boss. I have folk wisdom. Would you like any?

**MITCH.** What's your name?

**TEMPURA.** Tempura. Because I have been battered by life.

**MITCH.** And you're a vegetable.

**TEMPURA.** Ha, ha, good one. Well I have exhausted myself. Come, let us find Mr. Rick Shaw.

(**MITCH** *follows* **TEMPURA**. *The set does a big change, and it becomes Rick Shaw's Surf n Turf Nightclub and Gambling Casino.*)

## Scene 3

*(Rick's club. There's a bar. A piano. Tables. The décor is mostly red.* JOE *the bartender and* DAISY *the cigarette girl are there. [They are played by the Trenchcoat Chorus.])*

*(*TEMPURA *makes a grand sweeping gesture and addresses* MITCH.*)*

TEMPURA. Welcome to Mr. Rick Shaw's Surf n Turf Night-club and Gambling Casino. This nightclub part. *(makes sweeping gesture referring to the club)* That gambling part. *(points off stage)* Get drunk here, go lose all your money there. Make Rick Shaw very happy.

*(*DAISY *walks across the stage with her cigarette "box.")*

DAISY. Cigars, cigarettes. Have your picture taken with a monkey?

*(Enter* CORINNA, *a sultry woman, in an evening gown. She's very focused at the moment.* JOE *and* DAISY *have exited.)*

CORINNA. Tempura, where is Rick? I think he gave me a social disease.

*(sees* MITCH*)*

Oh hello.

MITCH. Hello.

CORINNA. I'm Corinna. *[pronounced: Kuh-reena]*

*(puts out her hand; he hesitates)*

You can't get it from shaking hands.

*(They shake hands.)*

CORINNA. You shake hands like an American.

MITCH. Do I?

CORINNA. Strong, simple, but with a slight feeling of domi-nance. Who's president these days?

MITCH. Eisenhower.

CORINNA. Oh yes. I remember him from the war. How long have you been in Macao?

**MITCH.** About 20 minutes.

**CORINNA.** I hope we Macao-ians are making a good impression.

**MITCH.** Yeah, okay. When will you be cured of your social disease?

**CORINNA.** Oh, later tonight. Tempura, get me my stash of penicillin laced with…well, you know. *(to **MITCH**)* I think I like you.

**MITCH.** Really? I try not to like anyone. Don't want to get tied down.

**CORINNA.** Or tied up?

**TEMPURA.** Oh, Corinna is an evil princess of desire.

**CORINNA.** Yes, I am. What's your name?

**MITCH.** Mitch.

**CORINNA.** Mitch. I need help memorizing my lyrics. Come to my dressing room?

**MITCH.** Sorry I have to find Rick Shaw and ask him about… Mr. McGuffin.

**CORINNA.** Ssssshh!!!

**TEMPURA.** *(same time)* Sssssssshh!!!

*(**CORINNA** and **TEMPURA** look afraid.)*

**CORINNA.** Want some advice? Don't ask Rick about Mr. Mu–….That man you said.

**TEMPURA.** Ditto, ditto.

**MITCH.** I'm afraid I'm going to have to. I'll be in the gambling casino, if you see him. *(exits)*

**CORINNA.** That was worrisome.

*(**CORINNA** and **TEMPURA** look at one another, scared that this topic has been brought up. They decide to sing.)*

**TEMPURA & CORINNA.** *(singing)*
McGUFFIN
MISTER McGUFFIN,
BETTER WATCH OUT
OR ELSE HE'LL RIP OUT ALL OF YOUR STUFFIN',
HE'S A DANGEROUS GUY
WHO MIGHT POKE OUT YOUR EYE

**CORINNA.**

I AIN'T TELLIN' NO LIE...

**TEMPURA & CORINNA.**

RUN HERE, RUN THERE
LAY LOW, DUCK DOWN

HE LIES IN WAIT
ALL OVER TOWN,
UNTIL THE COPS CAN CATCH 'IM AND CUFF 'IM,
LOOK OUT, LOOK OUT, LOOK OUT
FOR MISTER McGUFFIN

DANGER AND PLOTTING
RED BLOOD AND CLOTTING

**CORINNA.**

CLOTTED CREAM AND SCONES

**TEMPURA.**

HE EATS THEM
WHILE HIS VICTIM SCREAMS AND MOANS

**CORINNA.** (*overlapping voice*)

HE'S REALLY A SADIST

(*A shadowy chorus of two, in trenchcoats and fedoras, appears upstage. They are the* **TRENCHCOAT CHORUS**.)

**CORINNA & TEMPURA.**

McGUFFIN

   **TRENCHCOAT CHORUS.**

   RUNNING DOWN THE STREET

**CORINNA & TEMPURA.**

MISTER McGUFFIN

   **TRENCHCOAT CHORUS.**

   HE'S THERE AT YOUR BACK, AND HE'S
   PACKING HEAT

**CORINNA & TEMPURA.**

BE ON YOUR GUARD,
ELSE HE'LL KNOCK YOU DOWN TO NUFFIN'

   **TRENCHCOAT CHORUS.**

   BEWARE, HE'LL ATTACK, BETTER TO
   RETREAT

**CORINNA.**

HE'S A DANGEROUS MAN

**TEMPURA.**

HE'S GOT FRIENDS IN JAPAN

**CORINNA.**

SO BEWARE IF YOU CAN

**TEMPURA.**
McGUFFIN                    **TRENCHCOAT GIRL.**
                            McGUFFIN

**CORINNA.**
McGUFFIN                    **TRENCHCOAT BOY.**
                            McGUFFIN

**TEMPURA, CORINNA, TRENCHCOAT CHORUS**

McGUFFINNNNN.... POW!

*(They go into a dance. Then they conclude with:)*

**CORINNA, TEMPURA, TRENCHCOAT CHORUS.**

RUN HERE, RUN THERE

PACK UP, LEAVE TOWN,

HIS GUNS, HIS GOONS

WILL SHOOT YOU DOWN,

UNTIL THE COPS CAN CATCH 'IM AND CUFF 'IM

LOOK OUT, LOOK OUT, LOOK OUT

HE'S BAD WITHOUT A DOUBT

THE MAN THEY TALK ABOUT

**TRENCHCOAT CHORUS.**

MISTER McGUFFIN

**CORINNA & TEMPURA.**

IS PINCHING YOUR ARM NOW

CAUSING YOU HARM NOW

HE DOESN'T CARE

**TRENCHCOAT CHORUS:**

MISTER McGUFFIN

**CORINNA & TEMPURA.**

SO EVIL AND CREEPY

CUT OFF YOUR PEE-PEE

BETTER BEWARE

**CORINNA, TEMPURA, TRENCHCOAT CHORUS.**

MISTER McGUFFIN !!!!

*(THE TRENCHCOAT CHORUS disappears. Or perhaps exits.)*

CORINNA. Well, I wonder if people are going to continue looking for Mr. McGuffin. I certainly hope not. Tempura, I'm going to my dressing room and take some penicillin, and then a little nap...and then later, I hope I'll see that Mitch again. *(She exits.)*

*(CORINNA goes out one direction, almost immediately from another in walk RICK and LUREENA.)*

TEMPURA. Herro, boss. Welcome back.

RICK. Tempura, this is Lureena. I don't know her last name.

LUREENA. Jones.

RICK. I've hired her to be the nightclub singer here.

TEMPURA. Oh...you have. Well, we will see.

LUREENA. What does that mean?

RICK. Tempura is a typical Asian stereotype, he's very inscrutable.

TEMPURA. I've told you and told you!!! I am scrutable, I am very scrutable.

LUREENA. He's touchy, isn't he?

*(to TEMPURA, nice)*

I hope we can be friends, Tempura.

TEMPURA. Perhaps. The three-horned frog and the scorpion are sometimes friends, sometimes enemies. So we'll see. What's your favorite vegetable? Do you play icky wicky? Were you born in the year of the rat?

LUREENA. Broccoli. What's icky wicky? And I wasn't born in the year of the rat, I was born in the year of the ox.

TEMPURA. That's why you have great big breasts.

RICK. Do you like big breasts, Tempura?

TEMPURA. I can take 'em or leave 'em.

RICK. I'd leave them then. Take Miss Jones to the dressing room.

TEMPURA. Dressing room? Don't you want to...you know, talk to someone first?

RICK. Corinna? Listen, she does what I tell her. So tell her she's no longer the club singer, I want her to be the girl who blows on the dice.

TEMPURA. She isn't going to like that, boss.

RICK. That's not my concern.

(looks at LUREENA, moves closer, seductive vibes)

I have a new person to be concerned about. Lureena, do you have a place to stay?

LUREENA. No. I just got off the boat.

RICK. Well there's a furnished apartment above the casino – a small kitchen, a few small chairs, a great big bed – you can stay there for a while.

LUREENA. Don't get your hopes up, Charlie. This is strictly business.

RICK. Yeah, yeah, we'll work the details out later.

LUREENA. I like to work out details first. I get the apartment for free, plus a hundred dollars a week, plus some sort of per diem, plus approval of any pictures used for publicity, plus when it's over, I get to keep the plates and silverware.

RICK. Okay on the salary and apartment, no per diem, yes on the pictures, fine on the plates and silverware, and you promise to be very, very friendly.

LUREENA. I don't do anything I don't want to, Mr. Shaw.

RICK. And I wouldn't want you to, Miss Jones. I'm sure we'll eventually find things we'll wish to do together.

LUREENA. Well don't hold your breath.

RICK. I always continue breathing.

LUREENA. That's very wise. Me too.

RICK. Be ready to sing in a half an hour.

LUREENA. Thirty-five minutes.

RICK. You drive a hard bargain. Take her to the dressing room, Tempura. (Exits.)

(TEMPURA takes LUREENA to the dressing room area.)

## Scene 4

*(The dressing room. Table, chair. A small space, perhaps even just created by lighting. It should be downstage of the nightclub set, which should stay onstage, just not lit.* **CORINNA** *is there, getting ready to perform. Checking her make-up? Practicing dance moves? Doing vocal exercises?* **TEMPURA** *and* **LUREENA** *enter.)*

**TEMPURA.** Here your dressing room, Missy Jone.

**CORINNA.** What's this?

**TEMPURA.** This is Lureena.

**CORINNA.** Who is she?

**LUREENA.** I'm the new singer.

**CORINNA.** What am I?

**LUREENA.** I have a feeling you're the old singer.

**CORINNA.** Hey, what is this?

**TEMPURA.** Mr. Shaw say he want you to blow on dice now.

**CORINNA.** I'm a singer. I can't blow on dice. What if I inhale and swallow them?

**LUREENA.** Sorry to step on your turf, honey, but I need this job...

**CORINNA.** Not as much as I do. Look, sister, I'm gonna go talk to Rick right now. There must be some mistake. But while I'm gone, don't touch my make-up or my eye lashes or my opium.

**LUREENA.** I wouldn't dream of it.

**CORINNA.** Where's that bum? Rick, Rick!

*(She goes off, calling for Rick.)*

**TEMPURA.** Okay, missy, you onstage now.

**LUREENA.** Now? Can't I rehearse with the pianist first?

**TEMPURA.** I pianist, don't have time to rehearse. Everything in key of E, just follow music.

**LUREENA.** Well at least I'm dressed right.

*(The set to the dressing room disappears by magic or by stage hands. The nightclub set, which has been there all along, is now lit again. In the short transition,* **TEMPURA** *walks up to the piano in the nightclub, and sits down.* **LUREENA** *follows him a bit tentatively, not sure where she should stand.)*

## Scene 5
*(but the action is continuous)*

*(The nightclub again.* **MITCH** *is now seated on a stool by the bar. The bartender* **JOE** *is behind the bar.* **DAISY** *the cigarette girl is leaning on the bar, or somewhere upstage.* **TEMPURA** *is seated at the piano.* **LUREENA** *is a bit disoriented, trying to figure out where she is meant to stand when singing.)*

*(* **JOE** *makes announcement from behind the bar, talking directly to audience.)*

**BARTENDER.** The Surf and Turf Room proudly presents Miss Lureena Jones.

*(***LUREENA** *crosses to an open area near or down of the piano; a spot hits her. It startles her.)*

**LUREENA.** *(whispers to* **TEMPURA***)* What song are we doing?

**TEMPURA.** *(soft; whispered, mumbled)* pi-eey moo o' cow.

**LUREENA.** Pi-eey moo of what??

**TEMPURA.** *(still whispered, annoyed, enunciates better)* Pretty Moon over Macao.

**LUREENA.** "Pretty Moon over Macao." But I don't know the lyrics to that song.

**TEMPURA.** Make them up!

**LUREENA.** What? *(looks out to audience; wildly uncertain)* Well....okay.

*(Music starts…she smiles a bit anxiously at the audience, and starts to make up the song as best as she can…)*

**LUREENA.** *(sings)*
PRETTY MO-ON OVER MACAO
HOW BRIGHT YOU SHINE
PRETTY MOON, THAT'S OVER MACAO
YOU LOOK…JUST FINE

LOVLEY MO-ON, SMILE ON ME NOW
AND I'LL…SMILE BACK
SOMETHING SOMETHING…CAT GOES MEOW
MEOW…THE DUCK GOES QUACK QUACK

*(speaks)* At least I'm rhyming!

*(suddenly knows the real lyrics for a bit:)*

THERE'S A MIDNIGHT WIND A-BLOWIN' THROUGH
THE JASMINE AND THE TALL BAMBOO
AND LOVELY BLOSSOMS QUIVER IN THE BREEZE

*(though makes this one up:)*

THE CAT HAS FLEAS

PRETTY MOON OVER MACAO

*(bit uncertain again:)*

YOUR...YELLOW HAZE
DRIPS TO EARTH LIKE...CHAMOMILE TEA

*(chamomile pronounced "cam-a-meal")*

YOU'RE GREAT IN SO MANY WAYS

OH-OH MOON OVER MACAO
*(spoken)* I'm sorry, I don't know the lyrics.

*(**TEMPURA** pounds out the notes to get her back into the song.)*

LA LA LA LA... Brigadoon!
PRETTY MOON COME DRESSED LIKE A COW
THE COW GOES MOO MOO MOO MOO

ARE YOU MELLOW MOON OR YELLOW MOON?
BE SWELL, O MOON, EAT JELLO, MOON,
THE MOON HANGS IN THE SKY ABOVE MACAO –
    IT STAYS THERE !
MOON, OH MOON, YOU'RE SUCH A PRETTY MOON!

TEMPURA. Again!

*(**LUREENA** looks shocked, but starts over.)*

LUREENA.

PRETTY MO-ON OVER MACAO...
*(calls to **TEMPURA**.)* STOP!!!

LUREENA. *(to audience)* I'm sorry. I think I've finished sing-ing for now. I'm very sorry I didn't know the lyrics. This thoroughly inscrutable person refused to let me rehearse. Thank you for your patience.

TEMPURA. *(angry, yells at her)* A-Koo, a-koo! Sha-pie-a koo-puttibuh.

(**LUREENA** *goes to the bar and sits, a bit upset. She's next to* **MITCH***, who notices her. But she's not quite focused on him yet.*)

(**CORINNA** *enters, ready for performance. She enters into the spotlight. She has a Carmen Miranda-esque head piece on.*)

**CORINNA.** Ladies and gentlemen, I apologize for what you just heard. There's been a misunderstanding, and this woman, recently escaped from a mental institution, thought she was the new singer...but I'm happy to say she isn't, and I'm here to sing that old favorite of mine you're always requesting – "Mambo Malaysian." Tempura...

(**CORINA** *gives* **TEMPURA** *a signal and he starts* "*Mambo Malaysian.*")

**CORINNA.** *(sings, sways her hips a lot)*
IF YOU'RE GOOD WITH PERSUASION
FOR A SPECIAL OCCASION
I DANCE MAMBO MALAYSIAN BLACK 'N' BLUE

CUCCARACHA INVASION
IT CAN CAUSE YOU ABRASION
STILL THE MAMBO MALAYASIAN'S WHAT TO DO

HOW I LOVE TO SWAY MY HIPS
AND LOVE TO SMACK MY LIPS
AND LOVE TO CRACK MY WHIPS
WHEN I'M IN BANGKOK

IF YOU LIKE GIRL FROM CHINA
RHYMES WITH VAGINA
OH MY GOD, SO SORRY, TAKE THAT BACK

I DON'T WANT TO OFFEND YOU
I JUST WANT TO BEFRIEND YOU,
TAKE A CHANCE
LET'S MEET FOR BREKFAST
WE EAT GRAPEFRUIT AND MANGO
AND I TEACH YOU TO TANGO
NO, WRONG DANCE

BOY AND GIRL IS EQUATION
THERE MUST BE NO EVASION
SO THE MAMBO MALAYSIAN'S HOW TO GO

IF YOU'RE NOT TOO CAUCASIAN
ON THIS CHINESE OCCASION
DANCE THE MAMBO MALAYSIAN
YO CHO HO

EYE – Yiiiii – Yiiiii – Yiiiii !!
EYE – Yiiiii – Yiiiii – Yiiiii !!

WHEN YOU HEAR THE MAMBO BEAT
IT'S TIME FOR DANCING FEET
ALTHOUGH, OF COURSE
WE TRY TO BE DISCRETE
YOU CAN'T ESCAPE THE HEAT
MAMBO, IT MAKE YOU
NAUGHTY IN THE BED,
LOOK OUT, THERE'S MAMBO UP AHEAD,
MAMBO WITH ME !!!

(*CORINNA does a dance while the music continues.*)

(*RICK has come in to the nightclub toward the end of Corinna's singing, and is annoyed that CORINNA is singing and not LUREENA. During the dance, he goes over to LUREENA and talks to her animatedly, pointing toward the performing space where LUREENA should be. LUREENA resists, but RICK gets mad, and drags LUREENA back into the spotlight.*)

RICK. (*to LUREENA*) You're the new entertainer, so entertain!

(*to CORINNA*)

And your new job is blowing on the dice!

CORINNA. (*to RICK*) What's the matter with you?

RICK. (*to LUREENA*) I pay you to sing. So sing, damn it!

(*RICK goes to the side to watch, expecting LUREENA to obey him. The dance music to "Mambo" is coming to end, and just as it becomes time for Corinna to start singing again, RICK calls out "sing" again, and LUREENA starts her song at the same time as CORINNA starts hers.*)

LUREENA *looks a bit startled;* CORINNA *does too. They both start singing their different songs.)*

**CORINNA.**

IF YOU'RE GOOD WITH PERSUASION
FOR A SPECIAL OCCASION
I DANCE MAMBO MALAYSIAN
BLACK AND BLUE

CUCCARACHA INVASION
IT CAN CAUSE YOU ABRASION
STILL THE MAMBO MALAYSIAN'S
WHAT TO DO

WHEN YOU HEAR THE MAMBO BEAT
IT'S TIME FOR DANCING FEET
ALTHOUGH, OF COURSE, WE
TRY TO BE DISCRETE
YOU CAN"T ESCAPE THE HEAT
MAMBO IT MAKE YOU NAUGHTY IN THE BED
LOOKOUT THERE"S MAMBO UP AHEAD
MAMBO WITH ME!!!

WHEN YOU
HEAR THE MAMBO BEAT
IT'S TIME FOR DANCING FEET
ALTHOUGH, OF COURSE, WE
TRY TO BE DISCRETE
YOU CAN"T ESCAPE THE HEAT
MAMBO IT MAKE YOU NAUGHTY IN THE BED
LOOKOUT THERE'S MAMBO UP AHEAD
MAMBO WITH ME!!!
ME!!!

**LUREENA.**

PRETTY MOON OVER MACAO

HOW BRIGHT YOU SHINE

PRETTY MOON THAT'S OVER MACAO

YOU LOOK JUST FINE

ARE YOU
MELLOW MOON OR
YELLOW MOON

REMEMBER ME
BE SWELL O MOON

AND THE
MOON HANGS IN THE SKY

ABOVE MACAO

OH BROTHER

MELLOW MOON OR
YELLOW MOON

BE SWELL, O MOON
EAT JELLO, MOON

AND THE
MOON HANGS IN THE SKY

ABOVE MACAO!
COW!

*(The music stops and* **CORINNA** *and* **LUREENA** *both instinctively take bows.* **CORINNA** *feels annoyed and pushes* **LUREENA** *out of the center spot.* **LUREENA** *is annoyed and pushes* **CORINNA** *back. And* **LUREENA** *starts to leave, she hopes with dignity, but* **CORINNA** *runs after her and pushes her again…this time off-stage.)*

**CORINNA.** A-koo, a-koo! Sha-pie-a koo-puttibuh.

*(***RICK** *looks frustrated and runs out after them. We hear sounds of fighting off-stage.)*

*(***TEMPURA** *has been playing a bit of the "Mambo" beat in the background, trying to help.)*

*(***RICK** *pushes* **CORINNA** *and* **LUREENA** *back on stage.* **CORINNA** *is limping, and* **LUREENA** *has her hand over an eye.)*

**TEMPURA.** *(as if he is saying something charming)* Women! They belong in cages! Hope no offense taken by any of the women present.

*(Everybody stares at* **TEMPURA** *a little surprised.* **RICK** *grabs* **CORINNA***'s arm to take her offstage.)*

**CORINNA.** Ow, not that arm! That's the one she twisted.

**RICK.** Shut up! You're a nuisance!

*(yells at audience, a little grouchy)*

Everybody go gamble for a while, alright?

*(***RICK** *and* **CORINNA** *exit.* **JOE** *goes back to the bar.* **DAISY** *exits. Lights change from show time to a nice, late night romantic look.)*

*(***LUREENA** *is touching her eye; it does smart.* **MITCH** *crosses to her from the bar.* **TEMPURA** *is still by the piano, watching this.)*

**MITCH.** You doin' alright?

**LUREENA.** Don't worry about me.

**MITCH.** Nice singing.

**LUREENA.** Thanks.

**MITCH.** You want a steak?

**LUREENA.** I'm not hungry.

**MITCH.** I mean for your eye.

**LUREENA.** Oh. Forget it.

**MITCH.** I don't think a nightclub singer with a shiner is gonna go over too good. Tempura, get the lady a steak.

**TEMPURA.** Steak expensive here, boss.

**MITCH.** Put it on my tab.

**TEMPURA.** You don't have a tab.

**MITCH.** Well set me up with one.

**TEMPURA.** Okay, boss. *(Exits.)*

**LUREENA.** Just cause you're buying a steak, don't expect me to be nice in return.

**MITCH.** I won't.

**LUREENA.** Cause I've been around the block and back again. I know your type.

**MITCH.** You do, huh?

**LUREENA.** Yeah, need a shave, but good at sweet talk. Got big plans but no money, and you need a loan today that you're gonna pay back with interest tomorrow. And then you're gone.

**MITCH.** Well I do need a shave, but I'm not good at sweet talk. And I'd never take money from a lady.

**LUREENA.** Yeah? Can I have that in writing?

**MITCH.** Why don't you take that chip off your shoulder?

**LUREENA.** I think I better leave it there.

**MITCH.** At least put two of them there, one for each shoulder. Otherwise you'll walk crooked.

**LUREENA.** No one has ever criticized the way I walk.

**MITCH.** Let me see.

*(She looks askance at him. Then decides to show him her walk. She walks naturally, not too exaggerated. And her walk is sexy.)*

**MITCH.** You're right. Nothin' wrong with your walk.

**LUREENA.** Thanks.

(Enter **TEMPURA** with steak.)

**TEMPURA.** Here, boss. Cost 4 million chukunkas. I put it on your tab, with a tip for me.

**MITCH.** We'll talk about the tip later.

**TEMPURA.** Much later. When you dead. Hahahahaha. Just kidding, Tempura like to joke about mortality. See you later. (exits)

**LUREENA.** That was kind of ominous.

**MITCH.** Oh he's a good egg underneath. (a bit worried.) I think.

**LUREENA.** What are you doing in Macao?

**MITCH.** Oh, this, that and the other thing.

**LUREENA.** That's kind of vague.

**MITCH.** I don't like to talk a lot.

**LUREENA.** How long since you've been in America?

**MITCH.** 5 years.

**LUREENA.** Are you running from something?

**MITCH.** We're all running from something, baby, aren't we?

**LUREENA.** Yeah. I guess.

**MITCH.** How's the steak?

(She brings it toward her eye, but gets a whiff.)

**LUREENA.** Uh. It's marinated. I'll smell of teriyaki sauce.

**MITCH.** Still, you don't want a shiner.

**LUREENA.** Guess not.

(**LUREENA** eyes him. He's sexy to her. She puts the steak on her eye. He looks at her.)

**LUREENA.** Can I have some privacy while I bathe my eye in teriyaki sauce?

**MITCH.** Sure. I'll go get a drink. You want something?

**LUREENA.** Sure. A shot of whiskey.

**MITCH.** You got it.

*(**MITCH** goes upstage to the bar, confers with the bartender softly. Dimly lit there. **LUREENA** looks after him, takes the steak off her eye. She sings.)*

**LUREENA.** *(sings)*
SPARKS
I'M FEELING SPARKS
I FEEL A JOLT
ACROSS THE ROOM
AND GUESS FROM WHOM

SPARKS
I'M FEELING SPARKS
I WISH I WEREN'T
AND YET IT'S TRUE
AND GUESS FROM WHO

OH WHY DON'T I KNOW BETTER
I ALWAYS FALL FOR BUMS
WHO PROMISE ME A BANQUET
BUT ONLY GIVE ME CRUMBS
NONETHELESS
THERE'S SPARKS
SPARKS ACROSS THE ROOM.

*(He comes back with two shots for both of them.)*

**MITCH.** Did you say something?

**LUREENA.** No, just humming to myself.

**MITCH.** Oh. *(They both knock back the shots.)*

**LUREENA.** Mmmm, nice. *(hands him steak)* Here, hold this, I'll get the next round.

*(She takes the two empty shot glasses and goes to bar, and gets two more shots. Again the bar is dimly lit. **MITCH** looks at the steak, and then at her. He sings.)*

**MITCH.** *(sings)*
HEAT
I'M FEELIN' HEAT
I FEEL A BLAST
RIGHT FROM HER THIGHS
SHE'S QUITE A PRIZE

TESTOSTERONE IS PUMPING
I ALWAYS FALL FOR DAMES
WHO PROMISE ME FOREVER
AND END UP PLAYING GAMES
STILL THE LADY'S HOT
JUST LOOK AT WHAT SHE'S GOT

(**LUREENA** *returns, hands him a shot, holds one for herself.*)

**LUREENA.** *(sings; to herself)*
HE'S ATTRACTIVE, BUT HARDLY A GENT

**MITCH.** *(sings; to himself)*
SHE'S GOOD LOOKIN', I'M NOW ON THE SCENT

**LUREENA.** *(sings; to him)*
YOU'RE A TOUGH GUY, A MUG SHOT, A ROVER, A LUG

**MITCH.** *(sings; to her)*
YOU'RE DAMN RIGHT, I'M A WRONG GUY, A THUG

**BOTH.**
MIGHT IT BE US
MIGHT WE HAVE FUN
MIGHT IT BE HELL
THAT ENDS WITH A GUN
KAPOW, KAPOW

(*They both knock back the shots* **LUREENA** *brought to him. Music keeps up underneath.*)

**BARTENDER.** Last call.

(**MITCH** *and* **LUREENA** *looks at one another, decide no on another drink.*)

**MITCH.** *(to* **BARTENDER***)* No, thanks.

(**BARTENDER** *closes up the bar, exits.*)

**LUREENA.** Yeah, you're right. It would probably end badly.

**MITCH.** I'm bad luck for dames; and they're no good for me either.

**LUREENA.** Yeah, bad track record, both sides. Better not even try.

**MITCH.** Right.

*(Dance break. One of them is probably still holding the steak.)*

**BOTH.**
OH WHY DON'T WE KNOW BETTER
WE ALWAYS MAKE MISTAKES,
WE ONLY FEEL THE HEAT FROM
THE FAKERS, JERKS AND SNAKES
NONETHELESS
THERE'S SPARKS
    AND THEY FLASH AND THEY FLARE

STILL THERE'S SPARKS
SPARKS ARE IN THE AIR

*(They look at one another not sure what the next step is.)*

**LUREENA.** Well, thanks for the steak for the eye.

**MITCH.** You're welcome. *(starts to exit)*

**LUREENA.** Hey, what's your favorite color?

**MITCH.** What?

**LUREENA.** Come on, indulge me.

**MITCH.** Favorite color. I don't have one.

**LUREENA.** Everyone has a favorite color.

**MITCH.** I don't know. Brown.

**LUREENA.** Brown!

**MITCH.** You know, brown. Like bark on a tree.

**LUREENA.** *(liking this better)* Oh yeah. Well I like trees. I like blue, the color of the sky.

**MITCH.** I like sky. Goes with trees.

**LUREENA.** I suppose you don't like puce.

**MITCH.** What?

**LUREENA.** Just kidding. I also like gray with light coming through it. Like smoke in a crowded New York nightclub.

**MITCH.** Maybe it's nightclubs you like and not gray.

**LUREENA.** Yeah. My dream is to sing in a regular New York nightclub. And have one regular guy looking out for me. Paying protection money, punching any drunks who hassle me. That kind of thing.

**MITCH.** You mean a bodyguard.

**LUREENA.** No. I mean a fella. You know, a fella who cares about me and so ends up watching out for me.

**MITCH.** You look like you could punch any drunks you needed to.

**LUREENA.** Oh forget it.

**MITCH.** I'm giving you a hard time. You want love. Lots of people do.

**LUREENA.** Don't you?

**MITCH.** I try not to want much.

(*looks out, a kind of personal code*)

Dry socks. Roof at night. Nobody trying to kill me.

**LUREENA.** Dry socks. You've gotta up your expectations of life a bit.

**MITCH.** I don't like to be let down.

**LUREENA.** You're such a man.

**MITCH.** Yeah. Well, that's what the instructions that came with me said.

**LUREENA.** I'm gonna go to bed. Thanks for the steak. You wanna fry it for breakfast?

**MITCH.** Sure.

(*She hands him the steak.*)

**LUREENA.** Well, good night.

**MITCH.** Good night.

**LUREENA.** Good night.

**MITCH.** Aren't you going?

**LUREENA.** Oh yes. I forgot to send a signal from my brain to my legs. I'll do that now. (*frowns, thinks, "sends the signal to move"*) There we go. Good night.

(*She walks part way across the stage. He walks part way in the other direction. They both stop, look back. They look at one another, interested. And she says:*)

**LUREENA.** It's 1952. Not on the first night, mister.

(*They look at one another. Then exit opposite sides.*)

(*Substantial light change, dims almost to blackout.*)

## Scene 6

*(It's the next morning, in the night club, empty. A more morning light starts to come up.)*

*(JOE and DAISY start to come in. The sound of a rooster crowing.)*

DAISY. What was that?

JOE. I think it was a rooster.

DAISY. In Macao?

JOE. I think it was a recording.

DAISY. Oh. It must be morning. Well, good morning.

JOE. Good morning.

*(holds up a glass in his hand)*

Excuse me, I'm in a hurry, Rick needs his usual morning bromo.

DAISY. Oh, I like that Rick.

JOE. Yeah, you and 2,000 other dames.

DAISY. 2,000? Wow.

*(RICK stumbles into the bar area, holds his forehead. JOE heads over to him. DAISY's about to leave, but speaks to RICK first.)*

DAISY. *(cont'd)* Good morning, Mr. Shaw.

RICK. Don't shout, honey, okay?

*(She didn't shout.)*

DAISY. Sorry. *(she exits)*

RICK. Sweet kid, but noisy. Ooh the bromo.

*(He takes the bromo, drinks it.)*

Thanks, Joe. And if you see Corinna, don't let her know I'm in here.

*(JOE nods, exits. CORINNA enters from the other side.)*

CORINNA. Rick Shaw, I want to talk to you.

*(RICK's body slumps in frustration that CORINNA has found him.)*

**RICK.** It's too early in the morning.

**CORINNA.** How dare you hire another singer?

**RICK.** I said it's too early in the morning. Tempura!

**CORINNA.** Don't you love me anymore?

**RICK.** I don't know. You're all right. Tempura!

**CORINNA.** That's not very romantic

**RICK.** Tempura!

> (*enter* **TEMPURA**)

**TEMPURA.** Good morning, boss.

**RICK.** Take Corinna back to her cage, would you?

**CORINNA.** Cage?

**RICK.** Apartment, whatever, it's just too early.

> (*enter* **LUREENA**, *holding flowers*)

**LUREENA.** Did you send me these flowers?

**RICK.** Well, do they have my finger prints?

**CORINNA.** You again!

**LUREENA.** Oh good morning. (*to* **RICK**) I wanna make one thing clear. There's no hanky panky between us.

**CORINNA.** Now she's making sense.

**RICK.** It's too early in the morning for this.

> (*enter* **MITCH**)

**MITCH.** Are you Rick Shaw?

**RICK.** Oh God, what is this, Grand Central Station?

**TEMPURA.** No, boss, couldn't be, we in Macao, China. Ma-cow. Rhymes with Pow!

**RICK.** Uh huh.

**LUREENA.** (*saying hello*) Hello, Mitch.

**CORINNA.** (*saying hello*) Hello, Mitch.

**MITCH.** Good morning, ladies.

**LUREENA.** Ladies. I hope you're not lumping us together.

**MITCH.** I don't know. There are two of you, I just thought it was a fast way to say hello.

**LUREENA.** Too fast for me. Tempura, when you want me to rehearse, I'll be in my suite.

**MITCH.** Oh don't be so thin-skinned. I didn't mean to lump you together. Hello, doll, you're lookin' good. Enjoyed our talk last night. There. Is that better?

**LUREENA.** Yes, a bit. Don't like having to twist your arm for it, but it'll do.

**MITCH.** It'll have to do.

**CORINNA.** I'm not as fussy about hello's. Come up and see me sometime.

*(to RICK)*

You know, Rick, you're not the only man of interest here in Macao.

**TEMPURA.** Oh, thank you, missy!

*(She stares at him, baffled.)*

**MITCH.** Rick Shaw, I've been looking for you. I got a tip from a reliable source that you know how to reach Mr. McGuffin.

**CORINNA.** Ssssssssh!!!

**TEMPURA.** Ssssssssh!!!

**CORINNA.** Don't say that name! He's very evil. Rick doesn't want to talk about him, do you, Rick?

**MITCH.** I know he's evil. But we have some…business to finish. And I need to find him. Can you help me?

**RICK.** Do I look like the Missing Persons Bureau?

**MITCH.** Do I look like a chump?

**RICK.** In some lights.

**MITCH.** How'd you like a knuckle sandwich?

**TEMPURA.** Oh, he's always offering that knuckle sandwich.

**MITCH.** Look, I got some ways to make you talk. I understand you run a business in diamonds. Stolen diamonds. So I want you to help me or I'm going to the cops about you.

**RICK.** I was supposed to see McGuffin the other night, but he didn't show. I'm not sure where he is now, but maybe I can call a few people. Why do you want to see McGuffin?

*(Moody, jazzy music begins. Lights change. MITCH looks out. He's ready to tell his story.)*

**MITCH.** I first met Mr. McGuffin in 1949. I'd been bum-
ming around the country, trying to figure out what to
do with myself, when my friend Vince and I decided to
start a detective agency. We became private dicks, gum-
shoes. Mr. McGuffin heard about me, he had a job for
me, I met him. I've been trying to publish what happened as a short story, let me read it to you.

*(takes crumpled paper out, reads it)*

It was March, it was cold. It was St. Patrick's Day. I
stared across at Mr. McGuffin. He had bright red hair
and bloodshot eyes. He was drinking green beer. I hate
green beer. What do they do? – add food coloring to it?
What's the point?

He said he wanted me to track down some dame who
had double-crossed him and disappeared. He showed
me her picture.

Wow. Zowie. She was a knock-out. He said, "Her name is
Jane." I took his initial check, and started to look for her.
I looked in Chicago, Cincinatti, Chattanooga. I real-
ized I had started in the C's, and forgotten the A's. I
took a plane to Acapulco.

It was April, it was hot in Acapulco. Then I saw her…
wow, zowie. She dripped sex like water. And I was
parched.

We struck up a conversation. "How you doin'? Are you
Jane?" That kinda thing. I was falling in lust. She noticed.
We made love for days, stopping only for Mexican food
and margaritas. "Mr. McGuffin wants to kill me," she
said. We decided to hide out in an old shack I knew in
the mountains of Colorado.

One night I heard a cat meow, but we didn't have a cat.
Suddenly Mr. McGuffin was there, there was a gun
shot, something hit me on the head. When I woke up,
the police were there, there was a gun in my hand, and
Jane was dead. It made me sad.

The cop said, "why'd you kill her, buddy?" I said, "Mr.
McGuffin did it." He said, "Don't you know Alfred
Hitchcock calls his plots the McGuffin?" Damn Hitch-
cock, I thought – why do people know this kind of

crap? My lawyer was having delirium tremins, and kept saying, "you're gonna fry, you're gonna fry!"

I was trapped. Before the trial, I got on a plane and left the country. I can't go home, they won't believe me. So I'm condemned to look and look and look for McGuffin. It's a lousy life, but it's the one I have. The End.

**RICK.** That was the longest answer to a question I've ever received. You were framed for a murder is the short version.

**LUREENA.** I liked the long version.

**CORINNA.** So did I.

**TEMPURA.** I would've preferred a medium length version, with perhaps some dancing.

**MITCH.** So can you help me?

**RICK.** Like I said, I'll make some phone calls. I'll see what I can find.

**MITCH.** Thanks.

**RICK.** Now if you'll all excuse me, I have some diamond smuggling to oversee. And some bank fraud, and there are a couple of laundries I'm shaking down. I'll send Tempura to you if I find any information.

**MITCH.** Okay.

(**RICK** *and* **TEMPURA** *exit.*)

**CORINNA.** Rick is so interesting. He's always busy.

**LUREENA.** Uh huh. Anyone feel like lunch?

**MITCH.** I'd like to go to the automat. In Times Square. Have a cup of coffee and a piece of pie.

**CORINNA.** The automat. Oh I miss that.

**LUREENA.** When's the next boat?

**MITCH.** I can't go back to America, remember?

**LUREENA.** Oh. Right. Sorry. (*makes apologetic grimace*)

(*Lights dim on* **MITCH**, **LUREENA** *and* **CORINNA** *who go over to the bar area, and sit on stools. They're in dim enough light we know we're not meant to watch them right now.*)

## Scene 7

*(A balcony, or a pool of light.* **RICK** *and* **TEMPURA** *are there.)*

**RICK.** Tempura, get me Tommy Udo's phone number in the states. He may know where McGuffin is.

*(***NOTE:*** *Udo is pronounced "u-doe," a character in "Kiss of Death" 40s version.)*

**TEMPURA.** Tommy Udo dead, boss.

**RICK.** What about his brother, Timmy Udo?

**TEMPURA.** He dead too. Died in Sing Sing.

**RICK.** What about Ma Udo?

**TEMPURA.** She died in a nursing home.

**RICK.** Old age?

**TEMPURA.** She poisoned by head nurse.

**RICK.** Get me the head nurse's phone number. Maybe she knows where McGuffin is.

**TEMPURA.** Okay, boss.

*(***TEMPURA*** *leaves.)*

*(***RICK*** *thinks to himself. Then:)*

**RICK.** They seek him here, they seek him there,
Those Frenchies seek him everywhere!
Is he in Heaven? Or is he in Hell?
That damned, elusive…. Mr. McGuffin

*(Frowns, doesn't sound right; lights dim as he thinks, exits.)*

## Scene 8

*(The bar, immediately after.* **MITCH** *is seated by the bar,* **LUREENA** *next to him,* **CORINNA** *next to her.)*

**LUREENA.** You know, I was very moved by the story you told us about Jane, and what happened.

**MITCH.** *(acknowledging, but covered)* Yeah.

**CORINNA.** I was moved too.

**LUREENA.** I thought what you said showed a real sensitive soul underneath all that… surface stuff you have going on.

**MITCH.** What do you mean?

**LUREENA.** Oh the low voice. The stubble on your face. The pretending you don't care.

**MITCH.** I can't control the timbre of my voice or my stubble. As to caring, some days I care, other days I don't.

**LUREENA.** Oh.

**CORINNA.** You know, I suddenly need a hit of opium.

*(***MITCH** *and* **LUREENA** *look at her, rather startled.)*

I'm sorry, I didn't say that. I need to…take a little nap for a while. I have a busy afternoon ahead of me. Would you excuse me? *(exits)*

**LUREENA.** I feel so sorry for drug addicts.

**MITCH.** I understand it.

*(looks out, moodily)*

Dulling the pain. Distracting yourself.

**LUREENA.** Last night I think I misjudged you. I thought you were…you know, a bum. But now I think you have real emotions and feelings.

**MITCH.** No, you were right the first time. I am a bum.

**LUREENA.** Oh. *(feeling discouraged)* I wonder if it's too early to order a drink.

**MITCH.** Now? I thought you didn't approve of Corinna's little habit…

LUREENA. Well opium and a gin and tonic seem different to me.

MITCH. *(looks out, thinks of the meaning of life)* Addiction, alcohol, murder, hope, desire, despair. The world is a sewer.

LUREENA. Oh, you're so existential.

MITCH. So what?

LUREENA. Existential. You know...somebody who...gosh, I guess I don't really know the meaning of the word.

MITCH. How'd you even hear of the word?

LUREENA. I don't know. I picked it up from the zeitgeist. Another word I don't know.

MITCH. It's weird to use a word you don't know.

LUREENA. Oh well Jean Pierre said it. He was the French film critic I mentioned before. We hung out in Marseille for a while. He used to go on and on about Humphrey Bogart and Alan Ladd and the myth of Sisyphus, and God knows what else. He used to make me wear my hair like Veronica Lake, over one eye, and then we'd sit in the kitchen and hold guns. He was one of the few people I walked out on first. And he stuttered. But from the way he used the word "existential", I think it means...hopeless, pointless, but going on anyway.

MITCH. Oh, that I understand.

LUREENA. Well I was right. You're an existentialist.

MITCH. No. I'm just a guy. Who's kind of hopeless and is pursuing a pointless goal, knowing it won't work out but I gotta do it anyway.

LUREENA. Right. I see the distinction.

MITCH. It's hard waiting to see if I'll ever find Mr. McGuffin.

LUREENA. Yeah, it's hard to wait for anything.

MITCH. Yeah.

*(sings)*

WAITING AND WOND'RING
JUST WHAT LIES AHEAD
TOMORROW IS COMING
IT FILLS ME WITH DREAD
I'VE LOW EXPECTATIONS
BECAUSE OF THE PAST
I'M ADRIFT IN MACAO
  ADRIFT IN MACAO
AND TIME DON'T MOVE FAST

**LUREENA.** I know what you mean.

*(sings)*

WAITING AND WOND'RING
'BOUT SO MANY THINGS
TOMORROW IS COMING
WHO KNOWS WHAT IT BRINGS
I'M EDGY AND NERVOUS
BECAUSE OF MY PAST
I'M ADRIFT IN MACAO
  ADRIFT IN MACAO
AND TIME DON'T MOVE FAST

**BOTH.**

THE RHYTHMS DON'T SCAN
THE WIND BLOWS TOO SLOW
WE HAVEN'T A PLAN
WE HAVEN'T MUCH DOUGH
IT SEEMS HOPELESS AND BLEAK
CAN'T GET WHAT WE SEEK
WE FEEL CHEATED AND STIFFED
IN A WORD, WE'RE ADRIFT…

WAITING AND WAITING
FOR WE DON'T KNOW WHAT
WE'RE WAITING AND SITTING
IN KIND OF A RUT
IT'S QUITE EXISTENTIAL
A WORD WE DON'T KNOW
WE'RE ADRIFT IN MACAO
  ADRIFT IN MACAO
AND TIME'S MOVIN' SLOW

*(Enter* **CORINNA.** *Music keeps going underneath.)*

**CORINNA.** I'm so upset. I'm out of stuff!!!

*(Everyone is startled by her vehemence. Music stops too.*
**CORINNA** *looks embarrassed by her outburst, and what
she said.)*

**CORINNA.** *(trying to cover)* I went to my stash of op-...pan-
cake mix...and I'm out.

**LUREENA.** What?

**CORINNA.** Oh nothing. It's just I didn't have any...pancake
mix left, so I'm waiting for someone to show up with
some, you know, pancakes for me.

**LUREENA.** What?

**CORINNA.** Well, that's just to say I'm waiting, too.

**LUREENA.** Too?

**CORINNA.** Well I heard you singing before. And I felt lonely
and thought I'd join you.

**LUREENA.** Oh, well, sure.

**CORINNA.**

WAITING FOR PANCAKES
WONDR'ING WHEN THEY'LL COME
WITH BERRIES AND SYRUP
DELICIOUS, YUM YUM,
I THINK AUNT JEMIMA
IS QUITE UNSURPASSED
I'M ADRIFT IN MACAO
    I'M MIFFED IN MACAO
AND TIME...

*(starts to freak out:)*

God, it's moving so slow, I feel so anxious!!!

**(MITCH** *and* **LUREENA** *try to calm her)*

**MITCH AND LUREENA.**

RELAX AND SIT BACK
RELAX AND LET GO
LIFE'S ONLY A JOKE
IT'S ONLY A SHOW          **CORINNA.** This is comforting?

IT SEEMS HOPELESS AND DUMB
THAT'S HOW IT IS, CHUM
ARE YOU GETTING MY DRIFT ?        CORINNA. Uh huh.
JUST GIVE IN, WE'RE ADRIFT

**ALL THREE.**

WAITING AND TRYING
TO GET THROUGH THE DAY
FIND SOME NICE DISTRACTION
TO MAKE IT OKAY
THE FUTURE BEFORE US
LOOKS ENDLESS AND VAST
WE'RE ADRIFT IN MACAO
    ADRIFT IN MACAO
AND TIME DON'T MOVE FAST

(**TEMPURA** *shows up on another part of the stage.*)

**TEMPURA.**

LISTEN TO THEM, ADRIFT, ADRIFT!
WHAT BABIES THEY ARE, ADRIFT, ADRIFT!
THEY WHIMPER AND MOAN, DITHER AND DRONE

PUT 'EM IN BOAT, OUT TO SEA
LET 'EM ALL DROWN, GLUG GLUG GLUG
IT'S REALLY BIZARRE, WHAT BABIES THEY ARE

NOD HEAD, SAY YES
DO MY BOSS'S BIDDING
WATCH YOUR BACK, I MIGHT KILL YOU
HA HA, NO NO, JUST KIDDING

**TEMPURA.** (*spoken now, to* **MITCH, LUREENA, CORRINA**)
Tempura still love to joke about mortality. Pay no atten-
tion. Go back to your pathetic philosophizing. Tempura
go read soothing sayings of Buddha. (*Exits.*)

(*Music vamp keeps playing underneath, connected to
the song.*)

**MITCH.** I guess we were philosophizing.

**CORINNA.** I didn't think it was pathetic.

**LUREENA.** Neither did I. I mean we saw a theme between
us, and we sang about it.

**MITCH.** Right.

**CORINNA.** Right.

**LUREENA.** Right.

**ALL THREE.**
>WISHING AND WANTING
>WHILE WE WONDER WHY
>OUR DREAMS NEVER PAN OUT
>WE'RE JUST SCRAPIN' BY
>DISTRUSTFUL AND WARY,
>WE KNOW THINGS DON'T LAST
>WE'RE ADRIFT IN MACAO
>>ADRIFT IN MACAO
>AND TIME DON'T MOVE FAST

**ALL THREE.**
>THE FUTURE'S UNSURE
>WE DON'T FEEL AT EASE
>LIKE RATS IN A TRAP
>LIKE MICE EATING CHEESE
>
>IT SEEMS HOPELESS AND BLEAK
>CAN'T GET WHAT WE SEEK
>WE FEEL CHEATED AND STIFFED
>IN A WORD, WE'RE ADRIFT…

| **MITCH AND LUREENA.** | **CORINNA.** |
|---|---|
| WAITING AND WAITING | HERE WE ARE… |
| | WAITING, WAITING |
| FOR WE DON'T KNOW WHAT | JUST WAITING |
| WE'RE WAITING AND SITTING | WE'RE SITTING AND WAITING |
| IN KIND OF A RUT | |

| **MITCH.** | **CORINNA.** |
|---|---|
| IT'S QUITE EXISTENTIAL | WAITING, WAITING |

**LUREENA & CORINNA.**
>A WORD WE DON'T KNOW

**ALL THREE.**
>WE'RE ADRIFT IN MACAO
>>ADRIFT IN MACAO

| MITCH. | LUREENA & CORINNA. |
|---|---|
| AND TIME'S MOVIN' SLOW | TICK TOCK, TICK TOCK |
| TIME'S MOVIN' SLOW | TICK TOCK TICK TOCK, |
| | TICK TOCK, TOCK TOCK |

**ALL THREE.**
TIME'S....MOVIN'.....
          SLO-O-O-W

| MITCH. | LUREENA/CORINNA. |
|---|---|
| WE NEED A BIT MORE GET UP AND GO | LA, LA, LO.... |
| JUST HOW WE'D GET THAT, I WOULDN'T KNOW | BA, BA, BO... |
| WE FEEL CONFUSED AND STUPID AND SLOW | |

**ALL THREE.**
HOW WE ARE NOW
IS ADRIFT IN MACAO

*(They sit or take "waiting pose.")*

*(Enter* **TEMPURA**.*)*

**TEMPURA.** Now that you've got that out of your systems, I hope you'll go back to more constructive mental activities.

**MITCH.** Nobody asked for your opinion, Tempura.

**TEMPURA.** Oh so sorry, boss. Forget I say anything. Missy Corinna, someone in your dressing room with…

**CORINNA.** Oh thank God! Excuse me!

*(She runs off.)*

**TEMPURA.** I was going to say with telegram, but I speak too slowly. I follow her and watch her reaction.

*(Exits.)*

**LUREENA.** Telegram. Wonder what's in it. Maybe it's some wonderful surprise. What do you think?

**MITCH.** I don't know what's in it.

LUREENA. Well I know you don't. But it's fun to think of it, isn't it?

MITCH. Maybe it's a death in the family.

LUREENA. Well telegrams aren't always negative. Think of a positive thing that could be in it.

MITCH. Um. Maybe she won some furniture.

LUREENA. Won some furniture? What are you talking about?

MITCH. I won some furniture once. It was part of a beer promotion.

LUREENA. Oh.

(Enter CORINNA, holding a telegram, looking grouchy.)

CORINNA. That idiot, Tempura. It was some stupid telegram, and it's not even for me. (to LUREENA) It's for you.

LUREENA. Really?

CORINNA. I read it.

LUREENA. That was presumptuous.

CORINNA. It offers you a job somewhere else. Maybe you should take it. Excuse me, I'm happy to say my pancake connection just arrived. See you a bit later. (exits)

LUREENA. She's a drug addict, you know.

MITCH. Stop being so jealous of her.

LUREENA. I'm not jealous, I'm...just worried for her. Jealous. Shut up. Let me read this telegram. (reads it aloud) "Dear Miss Jones, I am a talent scout from the Ticky Ticky Tocky Club in Bangkok, and I caught your premiere performance in Macao last night. Even though you didn't know your lyrics, still I could tell you have real star quality, and I am authorized to offer you a job as a singer in our club in Bangkok. Whatever you are being paid, we will double it." Well, that's a surprise.

MITCH. You should take it.

LUREENA. Really? Well, maybe the talent scout is a nut. Or a white slaver. I mean, shouldn't I check him out first?

MITCH. I always go where the wind blows. No future for you here.

**LUREENA.** I guess not. *(slight embarrassment)* And I guess you don't mind the idea of not seeing me again.

**MITCH.** Look, I'm so used to being alone, I don't even know how to hitch up with anybody anymore.

**LUREENA.** I either meet the men who take my money. Or the ones who seem possible and then tell me to get lost.

**MITCH.** Come on, we've known each other two days.

**LUREENA.** Fine, but you're saying let's not do a third day.

**MITCH.** I have personal demons.

**LUREENA.** Such as?

**MITCH.** I don't know what they are, I just have them, ok?

**LUREENA.** Fine, fine. Well, I guess you're right. I should just go to Bangkok, and, I don't know, sing songs in nightclubs til I die.

**MITCH.** Sounds like a life to me.

**LUREENA.** Yeah, well, great. Guess I'll go pack. *(stands)* So long.

**MITCH.** So long.

(**LUREENA** *starts to exit.* **TEMPURA** *enters.*)

**TEMPURA.** Good morning, Missy Jone.

**LUREENA.** Oh shut up. *(exits)*

**TEMPURA.** *(calls after her)* How you like a knuckle sandwich?

**MITCH.** Hey, don't threaten a lady.

**TEMPURA.** Oh, she plenty strong. I come with good news for you about Mr. McGuffin.

(*Enter* **CORINNA.**)

**CORINNA.** Did I leave a great big glass pipe in here?

**MITCH.** No, you didn't. Could we have some privacy in here?

**CORINNA.** Sure, sure.

(*She pretends to exit, but hides somewhere on stage, listening.*)

**MITCH.** So what's this good news about Mr. McGuffin?

**TEMPURA.** Rick Shaw find him. And make contact with him already.

**MITCH.** He did?

**TEMPURA.** The evil Mr. McGuffin agree to meet you tonight – at 2 a.m. on the docks of the Shaway River in Macao. You are to come alone and unarmed.

**MITCH.** I'll come alone. But not unarmed.

**TEMPURA.** Oh you Americans so strong and brave, it frighten Tempura. *(screams, though somewhat softly:)* EEEEEEEEEEEEEEEEE!

**MITCH.** Be quiet. So tell Rick Shaw thank you.

**TEMPURA.** I will.

*(exits)*

**CORINNA.** Mitch, you mustn't go. It sounds too dangerous.

**MITCH.** I got a little tape recorder I can put in my pocket. If I can get him to admit he killed Jane, I can go back to America.

**CORINNA.** America. But it's much easier to find opium in China. I don't know where you'd get it in America. Why don't you stay in Macao with me, we can live in an evil den of iniquity, enjoying God knows what sensuous delights.

**MITCH.** Well, that's a tempting offer. You're a sexy dame. But...I don't feel right not being able to go home.

**CORINNA.** Oh, you're just like Dorothy in *The Wizard of Oz.* I wanna go home, I wanna go home. That's nobody for a *guy* to identify with.

**MITCH.** I liked that movie.

**CORINNA.** Well, sure. But then you grow up and you come to Macao.

*(suddenly cries for a bit; stops)*

I'm sorry, I was just overcome with sadness. Never mind. Let me go finish what I was starting. I wish you well tonight, Mitch.

*(Exits.)*

**MITCH.** *(to himself)* McGuffin – your time is running out. *(slightly worried)* Or else mine is. *(exits)*

*(Later that evening.* **TEMPURA** *comes back on, carrying a statue of a black bird. He puts it on the bar [or the piano].* **TEMPURA** *stands in front of the bird, and looks at it, grouchily.)*

**TEMPURA.** Stupid bird! Stupid bird! Ugly, ugly! Your momma!

*(***RICK** *comes in, and sees the tail end of* **TEMPURA** *yelling at bird statue.)*

**RICK.** What are you doing? Stop that.

**TEMPURA.** So sorry. Big black bird offend Tempura's aesthetic sensibilities. So sorry, if you like it. I work on liking it too.

**RICK.** It's a Maltese Falcon. It's supposed to have diamonds in it, only it's a fake. It has little pieces of corn, painted silver. But I'm going to sell it to the Countess del Leche right as she gets on the boat to go back to Bavaria.

**TEMPURA.** Ah, that a good one. She deserve to spend money on rotten bird.

*(yells at bird)*

Ugly fake, you going to live in Bavaria and be smashed into pieces for your painted corn.

**RICK.** Calm down, would you? You're giving me a headache.

**TEMPURA.** So sorry. You want your feet rubbed?

**RICK.** God, no, just leave me alone.

**TEMPURA.** Okay, boss.

**RICK.** What about that Mitch guy? Did you tell him I haven't been able to find McGuffin yet?

**TEMPURA.** Yes, those were my exact words. You cannot find him.

**RICK.** I guess he was disappointed.

**TEMPURA.** Very disappointed. But Tempura tell him many knock, knock jokes and cheer him up big time. Offer him foot rub, and he like it.

**RICK.** Uh huh. Don't tell me about touching people, alright? And I'll see if I can help that Mitch find McGuffin, but not today. Maybe tomorrow.

**TEMPURA.** I not sure Mr. Mitch still be around tomorrow.

**RICK.** What do you mean?

**TEMPURA.** Ohhhhhhh, I have feeling he going to be gone from Macao soon. Just intee-wishion.

*(Enter LUREENA.)*

**LUREENA.** Rick, I need to talk to you.

**RICK.** Tempura, give me and the lady some room.

**TEMPURA.** Okay, boss. *(to Lureena)* I saw Mr. Mitch talking real sweetie to Corinna, evil princess of desire. I hope it not wrong to tell you.

**LUREENA.** I couldn't care less.

**TEMPURA.** *(frowns)* You hard lady to bother. Oh – I want you to sing on-stage in two minutes, missy. *(exits in a mood)*

**LUREENA.** Yeah? You and whose army?

**RICK.** You look very pretty when you're angry, Lureena.

**LUREENA.** That's a ridiculous cliché, shut up. I'm leaving tomorrow morning for Bangkok. I've been offered a singing job there at double pay. I'm leaving Macao.

**RICK.** But this is your second day.

**LUREENA.** I'm turning over a new leaf.

**RICK.** But we haven't even slept together.

**LUREENA.** Oh grow up. And you can keep the plates and silverware. It's too hard to travel with them.

**TEMPURA.** *(suddenly at the piano)* Ok missy, you on stage now!

*(Spot light. LUREENA walks into it. RICK watches from the side. JOE THE BARTENDER shows up behind the bar, makes announcement.)*

**JOE THE BARTENDER.** Ladies and gentlemen, and now in her final swan song – I'm sorry, that sounds redundant, I guess a swan song *is* final…let me start over. Ladies and gentleman, and now in her swan song, here is Miss Lureena Jones.

**LUREENA.** *(sings)*

WOKE UP TODAY, THINGS FELT OKAY,
NOW THEY'RE NOT OKAY,
MY DREAM OF LOVE HAS SLIPPED AWAY

I'M FED UP AND I'M FRETFUL
AND I'M SICK AND TIRED OF MEN,
I'M ANGRY AND REGRETFUL
CAUSE MY BUBBLE'S BURST AGAIN,
SO I'M LEAVING TOWN IN THE MORNING,
MISTER RIGHT ONCE MORE IS WRONG,
SO GOODBYE AND GOOD RIDDANCE, FAREWELL AND
SO LONG

I'M EDGY AND I'M ANGRY
'CAUSE IT HASN'T WORKED AGAIN,
I'VE LOUSY LUCK WITH FELLAS
SO I'M GIVING UP ON MEN,
BETTER LET GO, GIVE UP AND GET OUT,
THAT'S THE THEORY OF MY SONG,
SO GOODBYE AND GOOD RIDDANCE, FAREWELL AND
SO LONG

I'M REVVED UP AND WIRED
MEN ARE PIGS, IT'S SAD BUT TRUE,
YOU CAN'T HAVE ROMANCE WITH A PIG,
FACE THE FACTS, AND THINK IT THROUGH,
SO FOLLOW MY EXAMPLE,
LADIES, TIME TO WALK AWAY,
WITH A MAN, THERE'S NO SOLUTION
THEY'RE DUMB APES, PRE-EVOLUTION

I'M GROUCHY BUT I'M HOPEFUL
TO BE STANDING ON MY OWN,
I'M BITTER BUT I'M HAPPY,
I'LL BE BETTER OFF ALONE,
AND TO ALL THE MEN WHO'VE LEFT ME
WELL I DEDICATE THIS SONG,
SO GOODYE AND GOOD RIDDANCE, FAREWELL AND
SO LONG
SO HOORAY AND HALLELUJAH
'CAUSE I'M MOVING RIGHT ALONG
SO GOODBYE AND GOOD RIDDANCE, FAREWELL AND
SO LONG

(**LUREENA** *exits. Lights start to dim.* **JOE** *and* **TEM-PURA** *exit. Scene starts to change, but* **RICK** *stops it.*)

**RICK.** Hey. Turn up the lights, would ya?

(*He motions toward the real show's pianist; and maybe even gives pianist hand-written sheet music. The band starts to play the music he gave them.*)

**RICK.** *(sings)*
THEY'VE GIVEN EVERYONE A SONG,
EXCEPT FOR ME,
THEY THINK I'LL HUMBLY GO ALONG,
BUT NO, NOT ME

I WENT TO OUTSIDE AUTHORS AND DEMANDED
THEY WRITE A TUNE FOR ME,
    SO THEY CAN MAKE THIS SHOW BE
            MORE EVEN HANDED,
I SAID TO THEM, I AM NOT AMUSED
IN THIS SHOW I'M IN, I AM UNDERUSED
I TOOK MY CHECKBOOK FROM OUT OF MY COAT
AND HERE NOW IS THE SONG THAT THEY WROTE.

I HAVE A SONG
I AM SINGING
IN A BIG LOUD VOICE,
YOU'RE LISTENING TO ME,
YOU HAVE LITTLE CHOICE

NOW HEAR ME HIT A NOTE THAT'S HIGH
I'LL HOLD THAT NOTE AND MAKE IT FLY
I AM TALENTED
WHY DIDN'T THEY WRITE ME A SONG?
WHY DID I HAVE TO PAY MY OWN MONEY FOR A
SONG?

NOW THE B SECTION,
I'LL TELL YOU WHAT SPECIAL SKILLS I HAVE,
I CAN JUGGLE
I CAN DRIVE STICK SHIFT
I'M AVAILABLE FOR PRIVATE PARTIES
WHADDYA SAY?
NOW BACK TO THE A

*(He motions off-stage for someone to join him.* **JOE** *and* **DAISY** *come on stage, seemingly pre-arranged, and sing back-up for him.)*

I HAVE A SONG
I AM SINGING
AND MY PITCH IS GOOD,
THE AUTHORS DID NOT TREAT ME
THE WAY I KNOW THEY SHOULD

> **TRENCHCOAT CHORUS.**
> NO THEY DIDN'T,
> BUT THEY SHOULD

I'VE GOT A LAWYER AND MAY SUE
I BET IN MY PLACE          **TRENCHCOAT CHORUS.**
YOU'D SUE TOO          YOU'D SUE TOO
I AM TALENTED
WHY DIDN'T THEY WRITE ME A SONG?
WHY DID I HAVE TO PAY MY OWN FUCKING MONEY
FOR A SONG?

      BUT LOOK,
I'M SINGING
IT'S ME
I'M SINGING
IT'S ME
LOOK AT ME,          **TRENCHCOAT CHORUS.**
                LOOK AT HIM

LOOK AT ME,

                LOOK AT HIM
LOOK AT ME!          LOOK AT HIM!

*(Lights go out.)*

## Scene 9

*(Outside the nightclub. A small area, maybe just a pool of light. LUREENA looking up at the stars. CORINNA comes out.)*

CORINNA. Hey, I was looking for you. What are you doing out here?

LUREENA. Oh just looking at the stars.

CORINNA. You mean in the sky?

LUREENA. Yes.

CORINNA. *(looks up)* Too far away, I can't see them. Hey, I heard you just quit and you sang some song about men are pigs.

LUREENA. Well it was a "moving on" song. I'm moving on. Gosh, it's almost two a.m., I should go pack.

CORINNA. Two a.m.! Oh that's why I was looking for you. Mitch is going to be killed. We should go warn him or help or something.

LUREENA. Killed?

CORINNA. Yes, he's supposed to meet Mr. McGuffin in the fog at 2 a.m. And he could get killed.

LUREENA. Well, you go warn him, I'm looking at the sky.

CORINNA. Wow, you're mean.

LUREENA. Am I? Well…of course, I don't want Mitch killed, but what can we do?

CORINNA. Go find him. And better bring some protection.

LUREENA. I'm sorry, protection?

CORINNA. Weapons!

LUREENA. Oh, I see. Alright. I have a small gun my mother gave me on my graduation from high school. It's in my room.

CORINNA. I have a poison blow dart. It's buried in the poppy garden!

LUREENA. Let's go!

*(They run off.)*

## Scene 10

*(2 a.m. The docks of Macao. The "Chase." Very much a musical number. Sounds of fog whistles, boats.* **MITCH** *enters, in a trenchcoat.)*

*(Also around are four shadow-y* **FIGURES** *dressed in trenchcoats and fedoras. They are not necessarily together [and are played by the actors who play Rick, Tempura, Joe and Daisy]. They are dangerous people, we don't know who. They are lit dimly, at least initially. Suspenseful music begins.)*

**MITCH.** *(looks around, calls)* McGuffin!

**MITCH.**

RUN HERE, RUN THERE
THE CHASE BEGINS
HAVE GUN, WILL SHOOT
HIM FOR HIS SINS

TO CATCH THIS MAN HAS BEEN MY OBSESSION
TONIGHT IT'S RIGHT TO FIGHT
WANT HIS CONFESSION

*(***LUREENA** *and* **CORINNA** *show up now, also dressed in trenchcoats and maybe fedoras.)*

NEED HIM TO CLEAR ME
WANT HIM TO FEAR ME
MAKE HIM BEG AND PLEAD
    AND KICK HIM
        SEVERAL TIMES AND MAKE HIM BLEED

**LUREENA.** *(overlap)*

THAT MAKES ME FEEL QUEASY

**MITCH.** Who's that? McGuffin? *(shoots in her direction)* Pow! Missed!

*(***LUREENA** *and* **CORINNA** *scream and duck away.)*

**MITCH.**

OUT OF THE PAST
AGAINST ALL ODDS
I'M MOVING FAST

     I'M PACKING RODS
     THE MAN I'VE SOUGHT
     WHO DID ME DIRT
     I WANT HIM CAUGHT
     I WANT HIM HURT

**LUREENA.**

     LOOK AT THIS FOG
     IT'S AWFULLY DENSE
     I'M FEELING SICK
     I'M FEELING TENSE

     IT'S LIKE PEA SOUP
     EXCEPT IT'S GRAY
     PEA SOUP IS GREEN
     WELL ANYWAY....

**ALL 7.** *(including the shadow-y* **FIGURES** *in fedoras and coats)*

     DANGEROUS NIGHT
     OUT FOR A FIGHT
     IN HOT PURSUIT
     GUNS COCKED TO SHOOT
     CARNAGE, BLOODSHED, AND MAYHEM!

**MITCH.** McGuffin! Are you there?

**SOMEONE.** *(using a gruff voice)* I am Mr. McGuffin.

(**NOTE:** *in production, we have usually had the male Trenchcoat Person be the voice, spoken into his head mike. And we usually keep him in shadows, or looking upstage, so that McGuffin remains this mysterious, we-can-hear-him-but-not-yet-see-him sort of person.)*

**MITCH.** Where are you?

**SOMEONE.** Here I am.

**MITCH.** I can hear you, but I can't see you.

**SOMEONE.** I can see you, Mr. Mitch. Pow, pow!

(**MITCH** *shoots back at him)*

**MITCH.** Pow, pow!

**SOMEONE.** Damn, missed!

**MITCH.** Damn, missed!

**EVERYONE.**
> RUN HERE, RUN THERE
> HE'S HEARD HIM NOW
> HE AIMS HIS GUN
> IT GOES POW POW
> IT'S VENGEANCE TIME, LOOK OUT FOR DISASTER
> WITHOUT A DOUBT LOOK OUT
> BETTER MOVE FASTER

**MITCH.**
> JUST NEED TO CLIP HIM
> JUST WANT TO TRIP HIM
> CAPTURE HIM ALIVE

**LUREENA.** *(to* **CORINNA***)*
> MY NERVES ARE ACTING UP,
>> I HAVE A HIVE

**CORINNA.** *(overlap)*
> PERHAPS YOU NEED LOTION

**MITCH.** Who's that?

**CORINNA.** No one!

*(One of the shadow-y* **FIGURES** *come forward.)*

**RICK.** It's Rick Shaw.

**MITCH.** Why are you here?

**RICK.** *(sings to tune of Rick's song from "I have a song":)*
> I'M OUT TONIGHT,
> HERE'S THE REASON,
> I'M SORT OF IN DISGUISE,
> I'M WITH THE FBI,
> AIN'T THAT A SURPRISE?

**CORINNA.** FBI !!! You are!

**MITCH.** Corinna, Lureena. Why are you here?

**CORINNA.** We were worried.

**LUREENA.** *(showing she doesn't care)* Not me. I just felt like a walk.

**SOMEONE.** Oh, yoo hoo – two men and two ladies. Ladies step aside please, I'm about to shoot my gun. Pow, pow!

*(Shooting is always "pow pow!" Everybody ducks.)*

*(NOTE: guns aren't used. Actors point their hands instead.)*

**SOMEONE.** Damn! Missed!

**MITCH.** Pow! Pow! Missed!

**RICK.** Ladies, if you've brought weapons, use them. *(shoots)* Pow! Pow! Missed!

**MITCH.** Pow! Missed!

**CORINNA.** Wait, I brought a poison dart gun!
*(blows through dart)*
Missed!

**CORINNA.** *(sings)*
> I BLOW THROUGH MY DART
> WITH ALL MY BREATH
> BUT DAMN IT ALL
> THERE IS NO DEATH!

**LUREENA.**
> PRETTY MOON OVER MACAO
> WE'RE SHOOTING POW POW
> PRETTY MOON, WISH I WAS IN BED
> DON'T WANT TO...BE DEAD

*(During the above, everyone moves around in slow motion, in a blue light. Then it's broken by the following:)*

**SOMEONE.** I'm over here, you pathetic posse!

**EVERYBODY.** Powpowpowpowpowpowpow.

**SOMEONE.** No, I'm over here.

**EVERYBODY.** Powpowpowpowpowpowpow.

**SOMEONE.** Fooled ya! I'm over here

**EVERYBODY.** Powpowpowpowpowpowpow.

**SOMEONE.** A little to the right.

*(Everybody shoots at everybody.)*

**EVERYBODY.** POW POW POW!

**EVERYBODY.**
> SOMETHING IS WRONG

WE DON'T SUCCEED
WE SHOOT THE GUN
HE DOESN'T BLEED
BANG BANG, BANG BANG
NO, MISSED ONCE MORE
WHERE IS THE BLOOD?
WHERE IS THE GORE?
WHERE IS THE BLOOD?
WHERE IS THE GORE?

**MITCH.** Let's forget the guns, and use our fists!

*(All five throw away "guns" and raise their fists. **RICK** and **MITCH** and the other men seemingly gang up on someone, through the magic of dim lighting or of something, we can't quite make up what they're doing. Meanwhile, the women – **LUREENA**, **CORINNA** and the **TRENCHCOAT WOMAN** sing downstage:)*

**LUREENA & TRENCHCOAT WOMAN.**

MURDEROUS NIGHT

        **CORINNA.**

        LOOKS LIKE HE'S READY TO
        PUNCH HIM

MEN LIKE TO FIGHT

        BREAK BONES AND GENER'LY
        CRUNCH HIM

**EVERYONE.**

PUMMEL AND POUND
RIGHT INTO THE GROUND
CARNAGE, BLOODSHED, AND
CARNAGE, BLOODSHED, AND
CARNAGE, BLOODSHED, AND MAYHEM

*(The men punching suddenly come to a realization and pull away, They see who they've been pummeling and pounding. Music stops.)*

**MITCH.** Wait! It's Tempura!

**EVERYONE.** *(spoken)* Tempura?

**MITCH.** It's Tempura. In a fedora.

**EVERYONE.** How odd.

**MITCH.** You're not Mr. McGuffin.

**TEMPURA.** *(Irish accent)* That's where you're mistaken. I am Mr. McGuffin.

**EVERYONE.** What?

**TEMPURA.** I am the evil Mr. McGuffin, who killed Jane Granger and pinned it on you.

**MITCH.** But how can you be McGuffin?

**TEMPURA.** You know how certain snakes can change the color of their skin to fit into their surroundings? I have that talent too.

**MITCH.** But McGuffin was six-one and Irish and had bright red hair.

**TEMPURA.** Exactly.

(**TEMPURA** *gets away from* **MITCH**'s *grasp for a moment and sings:*)

**TEMPURA.** *(sings)*

I'M ACTUALLY IRISH
YOU HEARD WHAT I SAID,
I'M ACTUALLY IRISH
MY HAIR IS BRIGHT RED,
I'M JUST A CHAMELEON
I TURN ON A DIME,
I'M ACTUALLY IRISH
AT LEAST MOST OF THE TIME

MY SKIN COLOR CHANGES
SOMEHOW I'VE THE KNACK,
IN SHANGHAI IT'S YELLOW,
IN GHANA IT'S BLACK,
AND WHEN I'M IN ATHENS
I'M ZORBA THE GREEK,
I'M MISTER McGUFFIN
THE MAN THAT YOU SEEK

WHEN I'M IN SPAIN
    THEN I'M SWARTHY AND SLEEK,
I PLAY CASTANETS

AND MAKE WOMEN SHRIEK,
WHEN I'M IN HOLLAND
    I'M LIGHT SKINNED AND BLOND,
I WEAR WOODEN SHOES
    AND SKATE ON THE POND

STILL THE PLACE THAT CAN MAKE ME SMILE
IS MY HOME, THE EMERALD ISLE...
AND I MISS ALL THE BLARNEY, YOU FIND IN
KILARNEY,
THE HILLS SPECKLED BRIGHT WITH GREEN
AND ME SISTERS JO AND JEAN,
BUT EACH MOMENT I'M WAKING, FOR HER I AM
ACHING:

*(becomes sentimental, very Irish)*

OH,
ME MOTHER KATHLEEN
ME MOTHER KATHLEEN

SHE'S GOOD, SHE'S A SAINT,
SHE'S A BONNY COLEEN,
AND SHE SCRUBS ALL THE FLOORS
AND SHE MAKES ALL THE MEALS,
PRAYS THE ROS'RY EACH DAY,
NEVER SAYS WHAT SHE FEELS

OH ME MOTHER
HOW HER LOVE FOR ME INCREASED,
MORE THAN ME BROTHER
SHE WANTED ME TO BE A PRIEST,
AND SHE WAS WAITIN'
BUT SHE WAS WAITIN' A LONG, LONG TIME,
I TURNED TO SATAN
AND A HEINOUS LIFE OF CRIME!

AND SO I MOVED FAR AWAY, WAS A VERY BAD BOY
AND DISCOVERED ME TALENT
WHICH I REALLY DO ENJOY:

THAT SOMETIMES I'M POLISH
AND SOMETIMES I'M SCOT,

SOMETIMES I'M FINNISH
AND SOMETIMES I'M NOT,
AND SOMETIMES I'M GERMAN
AND LIVE IN BERLIN,
IT GETS QUITE EXHAUSTING
THIS CHANGING MY SKIN

*(calls out:)* Key change!
ONE DAY I'M NORWEGIAN
ONE DAY I'M BURMESE
NEXT DAY I'M CHIHUAHUA
AND SCRATCHING MY FLEAS,
AND SOMETIMES I'M ENGLISH
AND SOMETIMES I'M THAI,
AT TIMES I'M A WOMAN
AT TIMES I'M A GUY

I LOVE MY MUTATIONS
BY NOW THAT IS CLEAR
BUT IT'S TIME FOR DEPATURE
WATCH ME NOW DISAPPEAR…. *(piano tremolo)*

**TEMPURA.** *(turning in a circle as he also exits off)*
Disappearing, disappearing, disappearing.

*(pokes his head back on stage)*

Poof!

*(A sudden flash of smoke. And the button to the song.)*

*(And **TEMPURA** is now gone.)*

**CORINNA.** That's the oddest exit I've ever seen. Did he explode?

**RICK.** No, he turned in circles saying "disappearing, disappearing." But when the smoke pot went off, he vanished for real. It's just part of his dastardly talent. We've been tracking him for years. Last time I got this close he turned into a mosquito, bit me and buzzed away.

**CORINNA.** I wonder if I'm hallucinating.

**MITCH.** Well at least I got his confession on my tape recorder. Oh my God. I forgot to turn it on.

**LUREENA.** Oh, Mitch.

**MITCH.** So it was all for nothing.

**RICK.** No, I work for the FBI. I always have a tape recorder on, no matter where I am.

**CORINNA.** Oh my God. I think I may need to get some tapes from you.

**MITCH.** But you got his admission that he killed Jane?

**RICK.** Yes, I did. And I think once J. Edgar hears the tape... you'll be free to go home, Mitch.

**MITCH.** Well, thanks. I thought I was going to have to kill myself.

**RICK.** And my work is over in Macao. So I'll be closing down the nightclub.

**CORINNA.** Oh. Gee.

**LUREENA.** So Mitch gets to go home. And I get to go to Bangkok. Goodbye, Mitch, it was good knowing you. I'm happy it's worked out for you.

**MITCH.** Thanks. I'm glad it's worked out for you too.

**LUREENA.** Yes, I'm just so pleased. I'm off to Bangkok, all alone. Unless – Corinna, would you like to come? We could probably both sing there – and I could work with you to help you get off drugs.

**CORINNA.** Get off drugs? *(incredulously)* In Bangkok??? *(doubtful)* Okay...

**LUREENA.** I believe there's nothing here for either of us.

**CORINNA.** No, I don't think so.

**RICK.** Well, good luck to you, ladies.

**LUREENA.** Goodbye, Mitch. I wish you well.

**MITCH.** Thanks, Lureena. I wish you well too.

*(Music to "So Long" plays as the two ladies exit. Played a bit poignantly.)*

**MITCH.** That's sort of a sad little tune, isn't it?

**RICK.** Yes, I guess it is.

## Scene 11

*(Sound of a train, or whistle of a boat.*

*Bangkok. The Ticky Ticky Tocky Club.* **JOE** *seemingly is there too, and he now speaks to the audience.)*

**JOE.** Good evening, and welcome to the Ticky Ticky Tocky Club in Bangkok. This evening in their first premiere performance – I'm sorry, that's redundant, let me start over…

*(starts over)*

In their premiere performance, here are…

*(looks off-stage)*

…no, they haven't finished their costume change, wait a sec…

*(slight pause; sings)*

Row, row, row your boat, gently down the stream….

*(checks off-stage)*

Are they ready? Oh good. And now, straight from Macao, here are Miss Lureena Jones and Miss Corinna Kockenlocker.

**(LUREENA** *and* **CORINNA** *come out, dressed in same fun, sexy costume together. They sing.)*

**LUREENA & CORINNA.**
    TICKY TICKY TOCKY BANGKOK
    WHAT A PLACE AND WHAT A CITY,
    TICKY TICKY TOCKY, KNOCK, KNOCK
    WHO IS THERE, AND DO YOU THINK I'M PRETTY?
    WHEN YOU COME ALONG TO BANGKOK
    HAVE SOME MONEY READY FOR THE KITTY,
    SO KITTY PLAYS WITH YOU
    SPENDS MANY DAYS WITH YOU
    TICKY TICKY TOCK.
    BANGKOK.

    COME TICKY TOCK AND TICKLE TOO,

KITTY LIKES THE MEN, IF YOU WANT TO KNOW,
KITTY THINKS YOU'RE SEXY AND SHE
LIKES WHEN YOU'RE BOTH PETTING

AND YES IT'S TRUE SHE'S FICKLE TOO,
KITTY LIKES A MAN WHO PITCHES WOO,
EVERYBODY LOVES HIS KITTY
SCRATCH MY FLEAS…PLEASE

*(They are joined by* **JOE** *and* **DAISY**, *now dressed as their Bangkok chorus.)*

**LUREENA & CORINNA** *(cont'd)*:
TICKY TICKY TOCKY BANGKOK
WHAT A PLACE AND WHAT A CITY,
TICKY TICKY TOCKY, KNOCK, KNOCK
WHO IS THERE, AND DO YOU THINK I'M PRETTY?
WHEN YOU COME ALONG TO BANGKOK
HAVE SOME MONEY READY FOR THE KITTY,
SO KITTY PLAYS WITH YOU
SPENDS MANY DAYS WITH YOU
TICKY TICKY TOCK.
BANGKOK.

*(They keep singing this catchy refrain sotto voce, and suddenly* **MITCH** *shows up.* **LUREENA** *looks surprised and leaves the song, while* **CORINNA** *keeps singing in the background, softly.)*

**LUREENA.** Mitch!

**MITCH.** Hey.

**LUREENA.** What are you doing in Bangkok?

**MITCH.** Is it alright to talk with you during the number?

**LUREENA.** Oh the whole audience is drunk, they won't notice.

**MITCH.** Well, it's been a while since I seen ya. And uh…Do they have to keep singing that?

**LUREENA.** Yes, it's our job.

**MITCH.** The tune's kinda insistent.

**LUREENA.** Well, it's catchy yes. *(to* **CORRINA***)* Ssssssssh!!!

(**CORINNA** *and the chorus are startled and stop singing, though they keep doing the number's repetitive dance step in the background.*)

**LUREENA.** So you're back in America now.

**MITCH.** Yeah, I got cleared. I got to go home. But I got thinking about you, and I, well, I had a question I wanted to ask. It was…

**CORINNA.** (*still dancing, but she speaks:*) What's he saying?

**LUREENA.** I don't know, be quiet.

**MITCH.** The question was…Look, I feel bad I said goodbye to you after two days. I'm sorry I didn't say let's try a third day. That's what I'm saying. Want to try a third day?

**LUREENA.** I've been reading a lot of mystery books in bed. They're very entertaining.

**MITCH.** Oh.

**LUREENA.** That's not a no. I'm just thinking… hold on. I'm thinking. Sure. I'd love to try a third day.

**MITCH.** Good. That's great. And remember my detective buddy Vince ? Well he owns this nightclub in New York City, and he's hired me to manage it. And I told him, I only know one nightclub singer.

**CORINNA.** (*while music goes on*) What about me?

**MITCH.** Well two.

(**CORINNA** *goes back to dancing.*)

**LUREENA.** So New York City, and a nightclub. And a third day.

**MITCH.** Yeah. Maybe more than three.

**LUREENA.** Oh, Mitch.

(*She smiles; they embrace. Probably kiss.*)

(*Lights down. Sounds of planes. Sounds of "America the Beautiful."*)

(*Lights up.* **MITCH** *on the side, watching.* **LUREENA** *and* **CORINNA** *and the twosome chorus in slightly different night club outfits now sing:*)

**LUREENA AND CORINNA.**
> NICKY NACKY NOCKY NEW YORK
> WHAT A PLACE AND WHAT A CITY,
> NICKY NACKY NOCKY NEW YORK
> HAIL A CAB, THE DRIVER MAY BE WITTY,
> WHEN YOU COME BACK HOME TO NEW YORK
> NOT TO DANCE ALL NIGHT WOULD BE A PITY,
> GO OUT AND ACT INSANE
> ORDER SOME PINK CHAMPAGNE
> THEN YOU POP THE CORK
> NEW YORK.

**LUREENA.**
> IS LIFE IN NEW YORK CITY GREAT?
> KITTY THINKS IT IS, IF YOU WANT TO KNOW,
> KITTY THINKS YOU'RE SEXY AND SHE
> LIKES WHEN YOU'RE BOTH DANCING

**LUREENA & CORINNA.**
> AND YES SHE STAYS UP PRETTY LATE,
> LIKES TO KISS AND THEN TO CONJUGATE,
> EVERYBODY LOVES HIS KITTY,
>> AIN'T THAT SO, JOE?

*(Suddenly an Asian dancer joins the line.)*

**LUREENA, CORINNA, JOE, DAISY, ASIAN DANCER.**
> NICKY NACKY NOCKY NEW YORK
> WHAT A PLACE AND WHAT A CITY,
> NICKY NACKY NOCKY NEW YORK
> WE ARE GIRLS IN COSTUMES ITTY BITTY,
> YOU CAN FIND IT ALL IN NEW YORK
> NYC IS KINDA NITTY GRITTY,
> SO MANY TREATS FOR YOU
> GO EAT SOME PIZZA TOO
> YOU DON'T NEED A FORK
> NEW YORK

*(When Asian dancer joins the line,* **LUREENA** *and* **CORINNA** *momentarily look suspicious, then decide it's okay. Then the song repeats, and* **LUREENA** *leaves the song to talk to* **MITCH.***)*

*(And the Asian dancer is, of course, played by the actor who played* **TEMPURA***.)*

*(The "chorus line" continues to do the repetitive dance step in the background underneath all the dialogue.)*

**MITCH.** Hey, doll. How's it going?

**LUREENA.** Oh good show, good crowd. Tell me, who's the new girl?

**MITCH.** Vince found her. Said her name was Billie Holliday Wong.

**LUREENA.** She looks familiar.

**MITCH.** Does she? Happy anniversary. Three weeks today in New York City, and we're still happy.

**LUREENA.** I know. Pretty promising, huh.

**MITCH.** Look who dropped by.

*(**RICK** comes in.)*

**RICK.** Hey, Lureena. You look good. Tell me, are you now or have you ever been a member of the communist party?

**LUREENA.** What?

**RICK.** Sorry, have to ask that of everyone these days. Say, who's that Asian broad in the chorus line with Corinna?

**LUREENA.** She's new.

**RICK.** Looks familiar.

*(**CORINNA** leaves the line for a second to say hi to **RICK***.)*

**CORINNA.** *(to **LUREENA**)* Cover for me for a sec, will ya?

*(**LUREENA** joins **TEMPURA**/**CHORUS GIRL** singing.)*

**CORINNA.** Hey, Rick.

**RICK.** Hey, Corinna. Are you now or have you ever been a member of the communist party?

**CORINNA.** Gosh, no.

**RICK.** That's good. You're lookin' mighty nice, Corinna.

**CORINNA.** Thanks. And I'm off drugs now, Rick. The more wholesome environment of America in the fifties has had a real positive effect on me. Also I've gone to a doctor for help. And he's given me these new things called tranquilizers. *(suddenly looks a bit dazed)*

**RICK.** That sounds great, Corinna. Maybe we should get married.

**CORINNA.** Wow. This is a good day!

(*Happy and engaged,* **CORINNA** *rejoins the line;* **LUREENA** *comes out of the line again*)

**LUREENA.** Is what Corinna told me true? You guys are getting married?

(**LUREENA**'*s comment is not triggered by* **CORINNA** *saying anything or pretending to whisper to her, it's a joke, a jump ahead transition.*)

**MITCH.** Well he asked her.

**LUREENA.** That's great.

(**TEMPURA** *leaves the line, and runs over to* **MITCH**.)

**TEMPURA.** (*as Billie Holliday Wong; girlish and excited*) Oh, Mr. Mitch, I can't tell you how happy I am to have this job!

**MITCH.** That's good.

**TEMPURA.** I'm grateful to you and Vince. And I don't know which of you is more handsome.

**MITCH.** Vince is.

**TEMPURA.** Oh I don't know about that.

**LUREENA.** Hey, back off, honey. He's taken.

**TEMPURA.** Oh, so sorry, I be good. Want to be friends.

(*goes back to line*)

**RICK.** (*looking toward* **TEMPURA**, *frowning*) You know, I can't stop thinking about it. That Asian dame looks familiar.

**MITCH.** Yeah. Kind of looks like a tall Irish man with red hair.

**RICK.** Yeah.

**MITCH.** Well, even if it is Mr. McGuffin, her legs are good and we need another dancer.

**RICK.** We'll just keep a close watch on her.

**MITCH.** Sounds like a good plan.

(**LUREENA** *kisses* **MITCH**, *about to return to the line.*)

**LUREENA.** Now you punch any drunks that start to come up to bother me, right?

**MITCH.** You got it, doll.

**LUREENA.** *(sings to* **MITCH***)*
> NOW KITTY'S FOUND THE GUY FOR HER
> WAKES UP WITH A SMILE WHICH IS REALLY NICE
> 9 A.M. IS COZY AND SHE
> LOVES WHEN YOU BRING COFFEE

**CORINNA.** *(sings to* **RICK***)*
> THIS IS THE LIFE WE'D ALL PREFER
> PUT THE SUGAR IN THE CUP AND STIR
> NOW SOMEBODY LOVES OUR KITTY
> SHE'S FULFILLED...THRILLED

*(**LUREENA** and **CORINNA** happily go back to their places onstage as **MITCH** and **RICK** look at them proudly and contentedly. The women join the **JOE** and **DAISY** and **BILLIE HOLLIDAY WONG** to sing the last chorus of "Nicky Nacky Nocky.")*

**LUREENA, CORINNA, BILLIE HOLLIDAY WONG, JOE, DAISY.**
> NICKY NACKY NOCKY NEW YORK
> WHAT A PLACE AND WHAT A CITY,
> NICKY NACKY NOCKY NEW YORK
> DO YOU LIKE WHEN WE REPEAT THIS DITTY?
> WE FEEL HAPPY NOW IN NEW YORK
> WE SEE LOVE IN BLOOM AROUND THE CITY
> WE'LL HAVE A WEDDING PLEASE
> FOOD COULD BE CANTONESE
> SWEET AND SOUR PORK
> NEW YORK!

**MITCH.** Hey, time for the sing-a-long!

*(**EVERYONE** holds up signs with lyrics for the audience.)*

**EVERYBODY.**
> TICKY TICKY TOCKY BANGKOK
> WHAT A PLACE AND WHAT A CITY,
> TICKY TICKY TOCKY, KNOCK, KNOCK

WHO IS THERE, AND DO YOU THINK I'M PRETTY,
WHEN YOU COME ALONG TO BANGKOK
HAVE SOME MONEY READY FOR THE KITTY,
SO KITTY PLAYS WITH YOU
SPENDS MANY DAYS WITH YOU
TICKY TICKY TOCK.
BANGKOK.

**BILLIE HOLLIDAY WONG.** *(a command:)* Again!

*(Everyone sings this one hundred more times.)*

**EVERYBODY.**
TICKY TICKY TOCKY BANGKOK
WHAT A PLACE AND WHAT A CITY,
TICKY TICKY TOCKY, KNOCK, KNOCK
WHO IS THERE, AND DO YOU THINK I'M PRETTY,
WHEN YOU COME ALONG TO BANGKOK
HAVE SOME MONEY READY FOR THE KITTY,
SO KITTY PLAYS WITH YOU
SPENDS MANY DAYS WITH YOU
TICKY TICKY TOCK.
BANGKOK!

## Curtain Call

# ADDENDUM

The silent Prologue that begins *Adrift in Macao* was written for the Primary Stages production in New York City.

It was meant to be like the beginning of a movie, and to give the ambience of the place, and to introduce all the characters. I think it works for that, and offers the director, designers and actors a chance for some visual fun. I also added the platinum blond who shoots her lover as a more pronounced nod to film noir. (She is a reference to Barbara Stanwyck in the memorable film *Double Indemnity* – the blond hair-do and dark glasses is meant to conjure up the Stanwyck femme fatale. In the film she doesn't actually shoot her husband; she seduces and convinces an insurance salesman to murder him for her.)

However, we had a much simpler opening in our previous versions of the musical – at a staged/sung reading at the York Theatre, at its first production at New York Stage and Film, and at its production at the Philadelphia Theatre Company.

In this opening, there is no Prologue music, there is no introduction of all the characters, there is no murder on the docks.

It just begins with glamorous Lureena walking off the docks, fresh from the boat docking, and she runs into Rick.

It's more playful and off-hand. And so I offer that other version here too.

## Scene 1

*(The docks of Macao, China. In the distance we see a woman in an evening gown, making her way downstage. Her name is LUREENA. As she walks, she looks around her, she's not been here before. She makes her way downstage, and raises her hand.)*

LUREENA. Rickshaw! Rickshaw!

*(None of the rickshaws stop for her.)*

LUREENA. Rickshaw!

*(A handsome Caucasian man in a white suit approaches her.)*

RICK. Hello, I'm Rick Shaw.

LUREENA. No, no, I mean rickshaw boys. Chinese taxis.

RICK. Oh, sorry. See you around I hope.

LUREENA. Well, it's a small cast.

*(RICK exits. A spotlight hits LUREENA. She sings.)*

LUREENA.
IN A FOREIGN CITY
IN A SLINKY DRESS,
THE WEATHER'S LOOKIN' STORMY,
AND MY HAIR IS QUITE A MESS,
I LOST MY LOVER BILLY
UNLUCKY ME, I GUESS,
NOW I'M IN A FOREIGN CITY
IN A SLINKY DRESS

MY OTHER CLOTHES ARE GONE NOW
THE HOTEL KEPT THEM ALL,
CAUSE BILLY TOOK OUR MONEY,
I GUESS I TOOK A FALL,
WHEN BILLY SAID TO KISS HIM,
OH WHY DID I SAY YES?
NOW I'M IN A FOREIGN CITY
IN A SLINKY DRESS.

GOT BAD TASTE
CHOOSING A LOVER

I SURE CAN PICK 'EM
IT'S SIMPLY INSANE

WHEN IT'S TIME
TO RUN FOR COVER
I'M LIKE A FOOL WHO THINKS IT'S SUNNY
WHEN IT'S POURING RAIN

*(Thunder, lightning.* **RICK** *comes back and holds a small umbrella above her head.)*

**LUREENA.** Thank you.

*(sings)*

I'M IN A FOREIGN CITY
IN A SLINKY DRESS,
THE RICKSHAW BOYS IGNORE ME,
SO WHAT, I COULD CARE LESS,
I NEED A JOB TOMORROW,
I'M SCARED I MUST CONFESS,
SCARED TO BE...
IN A FOREIGN CITY
IN A SLINKY DRESS
A SLINKY DRESS....SLINKY DRESS.

*(A clap of lightning maybe coincides with the last chord. The rain stops, it becomes brighter.)*

**LUREENA.** Oh, the sun's come out. How convenient. And I thought it was night.

**RICK.** It is night. That's just the moon. Welcome to Macao.

**LUREENA.** Thank you.

**RICK.** I heard you sing that you needed a job.

**LUREENA.** You were listening to my singing?

**RICK.** Well, I was standing next to you.

**LUREENA.** Some things are private. But maybe it's just as well. I'm a nightclub singer, do you know where I could get a job?

**RICK.** You mean as a prostitute?

**LUREENA.** No, as a singer.

**RICK.** As it happens, I have a nightclub/gambling casino; and I could use a nightclub singer.

**LUREENA.** Every country I go to I manage to get a job as a nightclub singer. I don't know how I do it.

**RICK.** You're beautiful.

**LUREENA.** Now, let's get one thing clear. I may be beautiful and even oversexed, but business is business, and never the twain shall meet.

**RICK.** Which twain?

**LUREENA.** The gwavy twain.

**RICK.** What?

**LUREENA.** I don't know what I said. Forget it. What are you doing out at the docks at this late hour? Up to no good?

**RICK.** In a way. I'm looking for a dangerous man named… Mr. McGuffin.

**LUREENA.** Oh, how odd.

**RICK.** Why, do you know him?

**LUREENA.** No. But did you know Alfred Hitchcock says that the plots of his films are just excuses for suspense, and he calls these plots "the McGuffin"?

**RICK.** Uh…. No I didn't know that.

**LUREENA.** Well, he does. I dated a French film critic in Marseille, and they love American B movies there, and they call them "film noir" which is French for… "black and white movie set at night, with danger and guns and glamorous women in evening gowns."

**RICK.** You're full of information.

**LUREENA.** I get around. Now what about this job you're offering me? Are you on the level?

**RICK.** Not entirely. But I am offering you a job. Come on. Let me take you to my casino, the Macao Surf and Turf Nightclub Gambling Casino.

**LUREENA.** That's a pretty long name.

**RICK.** And it's a long walk. We better take a rickshaw. *(raises hand, calls out)*
Oh, rickshaw, rickshaw!

**LUREENA.** This is where I came in, isn't it?

*(They go off.)*

# NOTES

Composer Peter Melnick and I had fun writing this show, and we hope you have fun doing it.

It is clearly meant to be a playful reflection of a certain kind of glamorous Hollywood movie.

Mitch is very much a film noir hero – he's gruff, doesn't talk easily, he keeps his secrets kind of hidden. (His back story of being hired to find Jane and then falling in love with her is a reference to some of the dense plotting of the film noir *Out of the Past.*)

However, I now think advertising the show as purely a film noir parody is a bit misleading. Lureena is not the typical "dame as trouble" in most film noirs. She is a "good egg," she's been threw a lot, she's a bit cynical, but she's a romantic at heart. And unlike the femme fatales in many film noir films, she is not destructive, she doesn't draw men to their doom. (By the way, there are some "good egg" gals in some film noirs – Lauren Bacall in *The Big Sleep*, for instance. But most people think of the "femme fatale" first when they think of film noir heroines.)

So I now prefer to describe the musical this way:

The show is a light-hearted, playful parody of two Hollywood genres: the film noir movies, in which the leading man is always mysterious and can't go home for murky reasons he won't say; and the less known "exotic adventure" movie set in Hollywood versions of China or Morocco or Trinidad. And in these foreign places, the leading lady can seemingly get a job singing in a nightclub no matter how well she does or doesn't sing.

The mysterious man Mitch is named for Robert Mitchum. And the nightclub singer who falls in love with him is named Lureena, and is a mixture of Jane Russell, Rita Hayworth and Ava Gardner, a wised-up broad who's still underneath a hopeless romantic.

I don't have time right now to write lengthy notes to directors and actors, as I sometimes enjoy doing. So let me give some more boiled-down advice.

I don't think imitations are a good idea. I've never seen anyone imitate Robert Mitchum anyway. And besides, my Mitch is an amalgam, he's just named Mitch as a kind of nod of admiration to that distinctive actor. But he's the emotionally covered, hurt-underneath-but-very-quiet-on-top leading man of many of those films.

More than imitations, I'm looking for people to embody the "essence" of some of those old movie heroes and heroines.

In line with that, I think there should be a definite spark between Mitch and Lureena. That's part of the fun of those kinds of movies, you start to hope they'll get together. Though the show is self-conscious about a lot, I still think it's good to play the love story with some actual feeling in it, not just tongue-in-cheek stuff. Obviously you can't get heavy-handed, and the Mitch-Lureena scenes have lots of laughs in them. But still I'd like the audience to root for them getting together.

Corinna is very much the "second banana" kind of role. ("Top banana" was a phrase for the main comic in vaudeville, and later the phrase was used for movies and plays too; and "second banana" was not the headliner, but the second funny one; and eventually it also came to mean the best friend or the girl who doesn't get the guy, etc. etc. And the role is usually funnier/ quirkier than the hero or heroine.) Corinna is jealous and seductive and changes moods quickly, and actresses seem to have a lot of fun with it.

Rick is not based on Rick in *Casablanca*. I called him Rick because of my silly "Rickshaw, rickshaw!", "I'm Rick Shaw" joke. Humphrey Bogart's Rick in the wonderful *Casablanca* has had his heart-broken by being inex-plicably left at the train station by Ingrid Bergman. He's also running the show in his nightclub, and he's smuggling people out of the country, and it's during WWII, and Nazis… and I'm sorry the name Rick and the exotic location has made some press people think Rick is based on that Bogart character. (I parody *Casablanca* in a section of my written-long-ago musical *A History of the American Film*, also licensed by Samuel French.)

Rick in *Adrift in Macao* is more of a second male lead, and he's a little sleazy and a little dabbling in illegal stuff, etc. And of course I play with his character late in the show when he realizes he doesn't have a song, and he leaves character to sing the song he got written for him specifically (by outside authors, he says). Somehow once he does that, the audience starts to warm to him more, and I find that at the end of the show the audience seems very happy that Lureena and Mitch are hitching up, and but that so also are Rick and Corinna.

Tempura. In a lot of these old movies set in exotic locales, there are no non-Caucasian characters with any significant roles. Or, as with the popular Broadway and Hollywood comedy *The Teahouse of the August Moon*, the one Asian character – a memorable one – was played by a Caucasian. On Broadway it was David Wayne; in Hollywood it was played by (gulp!) Marlon Brando.

The role that Wayne and Brando played was named Sakini, and he worked for his GI bosses who were stationed in postwar Japan. And he called all GI's "boss," just as I have Tempura often call Mitch and Rick "boss." And Sakini was wily and smarter than anybody; it was a very good role actually, but back in the 1950s, he was never played by an Asian.

I used "wily" and "boss" and mock subservient as my jumping off point to write Tempura. It was a lot of fun to write. And I was so tickled when the plot developed to justify (sort of) having Tempura sing how he's actually Irish.

Peter and I met through a mutual friend, and just decided to try writing together. "In a Foreign City in a Slinky Dress" was the first song we did together; and then we just kept going, and kept having fun. I'm hoping it's fun for you to work on.

Best, Chris Durang, March 2009

From the Reviews of
## ADRIFT IN MACAO...

"And there are, of course, those songs...Melnick demonstrates an affinity for melody and old-fashioned showmanship that link him to his grandfather, Richard Rodgers..."
- Matthew Murray, Talkin' Broadway.com

"... with a drop-dead funny book and shamefully silly lyrics by Christopher Durang and lethally catchy music by Peter Melnick. *A Drift In Macao* lovingly parodies the Hollywood film noir classics of the 1940's and 50's..."
- Michael Dale, Broadwayworld.com

Also by
Christopher Durang...

Beyond Therapy

A History of the American Film

Miss Witherspoon

Mrs. Bob Cratchit's Wild
Christmas Binge

Please visit our website **samuelfrench.com** for complete
descriptions and licensing information

Breinigsville, PA USA
23 February 2010
232972BV00005B/35/P